"I am aware," said the intruder composedly, "that you have many trick inventions in here, but no one of them could overpower me quickly enough to prevent me from dropping this nitroglycerin. In fact, even if I were struck instantly dead, in my falling would come your destruction. So stay right where you are while I walk out with that painting!"

"Aren't you taking desperate risks just to get hold of a fake?" The Avenger suggested.

"A fake, really?" Harris replied with indifference. "Regardless, I'll have it. Don't move."

This thief risked his life for a picture he knew was worthless. "This is no simple art theft," mused the Avenger. At stake might indeed be **PICTURES OF DEATH.**

Published By

WARNER PAPERBACK LIBRARY

PICTURES OF DEATH

by Kenneth Robeson

WARNER
PAPERBACK
LIBRARY

A Warner Communications Company

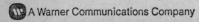

PICTURES
OF DEATH

CHAPTER I

A Long Way Down

The whole thing boiled down to just this: if a little boy's nose had not been red, the whole history of the United States of America might have been changed.

That statement is made after due thought and after consideration of a great many sinister and complicated factors.

Algernon Heathcote Smith and Nellie Gray, however, were thinking little of noses and not at all of history at the time. They were having fun without violence, which was very rare for anyone connected with The Avenger as these two were. To The Avenger and his aids, that band of crime fighters whose names were synonymous with terror to the underworld, fun was something usually associated with gunplay, automobile crashes and the sweet feel of fists buried deep in ratlike faces.

But this night, these two were having fun just as ordinary people might. They were dancing at the Pink Room of the Coyle Hotel in New York.

Smitty and Nellie, as a couple, had to be seen to be believed.

Algernon Heathcote Smith—a name no one ever called him, save in peril of his life—was a giant. He was six feet nine inches tall, weighed nearly three hundred solid pounds and had such a vast chest that his arms couldn't hang down straight.

Nellie Gray, on the other hand, was barely five feet high, weighed about an even hundred pounds and was as dainty and blonde and demure as a porcelain statuette.

The two had a table near the window, which was forty-four floors above the Manhattan streets, and were waiting impatiently for the orchestra to start playing again. They wanted to dance; they liked to dance. And if anybody felt like grinning at dainty five feet dancing with six feet nine, well, let him grin.

They were waiting impatiently for the music; but neither one would have been caught dead admitting that to the other. The only remarks they gave each other were calculated insults.

"You were always the worst dancer in town," said Nellie sweetly. "But just lately you've gone downhill even from that status. I'll be wearing size six shoes after tonight."

Inasmuch as little Nellie wore size threes ordinarily, there was a considerable amount of acid in the remark.

"Yeah?" growled Smitty, stung. "You've noticed everyone looking at us, haven't you? That's because we make such a picture on the dance floor. And the reason we make it is me."

"Picture?" murmured Nellie, looking up to Smitty's vast height, and to his moonlike face with its bland, china-blue eyes. "A whole mural, I'd say."

"There you go. Just because I'm a little oversize—"

"Would you say that Gargantua was a bit oversize?" she inquired.

"O.K., O.K.," said Smitty. "But there have been times

when you didn't mind my size. Whenever you go out and get yourself in some jam because you leap before you look, and when I have to come to your rescue, you like it."

Now it was Nellie's turn to be stung.

Everyone connected with The Avenger, because of the terrible danger of his work, was frequently getting into deadly predicaments, which meant that the others dropped everything to come to the rescue. It just happened that Smitty had hauled Nellie out of trouble by the scruff of her pretty neck oftener than he had anyone else. Which burned Nellie up.

"Listen, you behemoth—" she began.

But then two things stopped them. One was the beginning of music for the next dance. The other, as they both rose, was the approach of a curious-looking man to their table.

The man was enormously fat. Though he was a foot shorter than the gigantic Smitty, he must have weighed nearly as much. He was very dark, too, with the type of beard that needs attention twice a day. The folds of flesh making up his blue jowls were constantly set in a beaming smile that was belied by his eyes.

His eyes were small and glittering black; and they looked at everything and everybody with a mean sort of concentration, as if wondering what profit could be squeezed out of that.

"Pardon me," the fat man said. "You are Mr. Smith and Miss Gray, I believe."

"That's right," said Smitty, itching to whirl his diminutive partner to the music. He was never to enjoy that particular dance, however.

"You are friends of Mr. Richard Benson?"

Friends was a mild term, but Smitty let it go. He merely nodded. Also, he reflected that there was a slight accent in the man's words. French, he thought. But a very cosmopolitan Frenchman, because the man's English was perfect.

The fat man looked around as if to make sure no one could overhear. He was safe. Everyone from the near tables was out on the dance floor.

"I have an object to sell," he said in a low tone, "that I am sure would interest Mr. Benson. But I have been unable to get in touch with him about it."

Little Nellie flicked a glance at big Smitty. This had a phony sound. Dick Benson, The Avenger, was a very approachable man. He had to be; his business was helping people in distress whose troubles went beyond normal police ability. Therefore, he was "in" to most callers. When a man like this fat guy said he'd been unable to contact The Avenger, even to sell something, it sounded fishy.

But neither of them let on. They just looked interested.

"Perhaps," said the enormously fat man, "you would . . . er . . . present this object to him and see if he would care to purchase it."

"Perhaps we would," said Nellie evenly. "But we'd like to know a few things first."

"But naturally," said the fat man.

"Who are you?"

"I am Frank Teebo."

Smitty decided it was more likely François Thebaud.

"What are you?" said Nellie to the fat man.

"I am an artists' agent. I had an office in Paris till the war started."

"What are we to present for Mr. Benson's inspection?"

"A painting," said Teebo.

"What painting?"

Teebo glanced around again. When he finally answered, it was in a tone so furtive that even Smitty and Nellie could scarcely hear.

" 'The Dock,' by Gauguin," Teebo breathed.

Smitty checked a whistle of astonishment.

The giant, with his moonface and blue eyes and air of vast good nature, looked dumb. Actually, he was far from that. He was an electrical engineer with a brilliant reputation, with a string of radio inventions to his credit. Besides, he was unusually well informed on a score of other subjects.

One of these subjects was art.

Smitty knew something about the painting called "The Dock." It was a picture of a wharf at Villefranche, on France's Mediterranean coast near Nice. One of Gauguin's best, it had been in a private collection in Paris the last Smitty had heard of it.

It was worth probably a hundred thousand dollars.

"How," the giant demanded, blue eyes not looking quite so bland and innocent as usual, "do you happen to be in this country with a picture like 'The Dock'?"

Teebo looked around again. The move had a comic quality. But the next few minutes were to prove that there was nothing comic whatever about his apprehensions.

"In war, there is much looting," he whispered. "Many art treasures get into strange hands. 'The Dock' got into mine. I have learned that your Mr. Benson is immensely wealthy and is a well-known art collector. So I thought—"

It was Nellie who made up their minds for them. What the man had said about The Avenger was true.

A man whose life was dedicated to stamping out crime, Dick Benson had his softer moments. One of these concerned great paintings. He loved them and could afford them. If this fat fellow really had Gauguin's "Dock" to sell, Benson would undoubtedly buy it. After the war was over, he'd probably give it back to stricken France as a gift; but meanwhile he'd have had the enjoyment of it.

"We'll look at it," nodded Nellie.

Smitty sighed and called for the check.

"Where is the picture?" asked Nellie.

"At my shop on Eighty-ninth Street," said Teebo.

Smitty loomed comically beside dainty Nellie Gray

11

as they walked to the entrance of the Pink Room with balloonlike Teebo.

"Where's your shop, exactly?" Smitty demanded.

"That, I'll not say. I will lead you to it; and, in the taxi, you must keep your head down for the last few blocks in order not to see."

"Oh! So it's like that!"

"What difference does it make if you don't see exactly where my shop is?" said the fat man hastily. "You won't mind, I am sure. It doesn't look like an art shop, but in it is 'The Dock.' I guarantee."

"Wait'll I get my hat," said Smitty, turning toward the checkroom.

"I'll powder my nose," Nellie decided.

And in such manner was a man doomed to die.

As has been said, the Pink Room is on the forty-fourth floor of the Coyle Hotel. On the side where the supper club itself extends, there is a drop of twenty stories to a setback. On the side containing the foyer, checkrooms and lounges, there is no setback. It is forty-four stories straight down to the sidewalk.

That, if anyone should ask you, is a long, long way down!

When Smitty and Nellie went their separate ways, Teebo nervously walked to a window. The view from there over Manhattan's electrically lighted expanse was gorgeous. But it is doubtful if Teebo noticed the view. He just stood at the window—and looked scared.

Then Teebo wasn't there any more.

The window was open to let all possible cool air in, because this was midsummer and a hot night. It was open wide enough for even a man as wide as Teebo to step out of it. But then no one would be insane enough to step out of a window into forty-four floors of thin air, would he? Of course not.

Yet, the fact remained that at one moment Teebo

stood looking out the open window—and at the next there was just the open window with no one at it.

The first to notice was a woman in a white evening frock, cut so low that even the head waiter stared in fascination. And she wasn't sure of the disappearance.

"That man," she said in a startled tone to the sleek dark chap who was her escort.

"What man?" the escort said.

"The fat man. Where on earth did he go?"

"What are you talking about? I don't see a fat man."

"That's just it." Fear was creeping into the woman's voice. "He was standing by that open window. I looked away, looked back again, and he wasn't there."

"Probably just went to the men's lounge," said her companion indifferently.

"No, he couldn't have. I mean, I only looked away a second, not long enough for him to have moved more than a few steps—"

She stopped. The two of them bent their heads to listen. From far below came a faint, humming sound. But faint as it was, there was excitement in it.

The hum came from a rapidly growing crowd that gathered around something that had fallen so far and so hard that it had cracked the solid sidewalk in a dozen places.

CHAPTER II

Get That Picture!

"The guy was crazy," Smitty concluded.

Nellie said nothing. She just looked thoughtful.

"He must have been," said Smitty. "There's no other way to explain it. He wants us to get a picture and take it to the chief to see if he wants to buy it. Then, having won his point, what does he do? He steps out of a window. Just plain nuts."

"Did he step from the window?" demanded Nellie. "Or was he pushed?"

"Who was around to push him?" shrugged Smitty.

Nellie went to the couple who had first noticed the disappearance. Or, rather, the woman in white.

The place was an overturned beehive, by now. And all the excitement gave Nellie her chance. The woman in white was in a sad state of shock, and the crowd made it worse.

"Back," Nellie said, with an air of authority that outweighed her diminutive size. "Can't you see she's about to faint? Stand back! You," she added to the dark, sleek escort, "help me get her to the lounge."

In the women's lounge, with the door barred, Nellie tried some questions while she chafed the woman's wrists and put cold water on her forehead.

"Did you see him jump?" she asked.

The woman shivered.

"I saw him standing there," she said. "Then I didn't see him. That was all."

"Did you see anyone near him?"

"No. There wasn't a soul."

"There's a ledge outside the window," Nellie observed. "Not a very wide one, but I suppose someone could stand on it. If anyone had been out there, could you have seen him?"

"I . . . I think so. I'm not sure."

"What's the idea of all the questions?" demanded the man angrily. "Are you a police woman or something?"

"Call it something," said Nellie crisply. She transferred her attention to him.

He was of average height, a bit heavy, with dark, sleek hair and a good-naturedly dissipated face. A rather weak face even in anger. The term "playboy" was coined to fit such a person.

"You saw nothing?" Nellie said.

"Not one thing. I think you'd better let us alone."

"What's your name, if you don't mind the question?"

"I do mind," snapped the man. "Not that I have anything to hide, though— Oh, well, my name's Richard Addington. This is Miss Emily Brace."

Nellie nodded. "How far were you two from the fat man?"

"About twenty feet," said Addington.

The woman in white was breathing more evenly and seemed to be feeling better. Nellie thought she had all

16

the information out of the two that there was to be had. Which was nothing.

"You two had better stay till the police get up here," she said. And she left.

Smitty was by the elevators when she got back to the foyer. A door opened. They got in and went down.

"Know what I think?" said the giant. "We'd better go to this guy Teebo's art shop and look around."

"Sure," said Nellie. "He tries to sell us a picture and zingo! He's murdered. There must be a connection. But how are we to find his place? All he said was that it was on Eighty-ninth Street and that it didn't look like an art shop. There's an awful lot of Eighty-ninth Street."

"Maybe there'll be an answer downstairs," shrugged the big fellow.

There was.

The crowd around the tragic, flattened figure on the sidewalk had grown even bigger, but Smitty was born to cut through crowds. He plowed along like a tank, while Nellie went behind him like a dainty yacht protected from storm by the lee of a huge ocean liner.

They got to the police ring, and the police nodded respectfully. All of them knew The Avenger's aides.

"What's the dope?" demanded Smitty.

"Little enough, Mr. Smith," said a lieutenant. "Some of the boys are on the way up to the Pink Room now to see what they can find. On this end we have learned only two things. The guy's name was Teebo, and he was awful fat." Even the lieutenant shuddered.

"Nothing in his pockets?" said Smitty.

"A slip of paper with a number on it," said the man. "The number might be anything—phone number, address without a street being named so that it might be in any town in the United States, anything."

"Could I see that?" said Smitty.

The lieutenant showed him a slip of paper. It was part of a cigarette package, the plain inside bit of the paper bearing the number. Smitty kept Nellie from seeing the paper. It was sopped with red.

The number was 87-89.

"Thanks," said Smitty.

He backed out of the crowd, with Nellie in tow.

Teebo had suggested going to his shop in a taxi, and Smitty and Nellie had agreed. But they had a car of their own there. Or, rather, one of The Avenger's fleet of cars, since all the property of this indomitable band was, in a sense, owned by the whole group and used as any one of them pleased.

They got into it, a long, tubelike coupe. Nellie said, "You think that's the address on Eighty-ninth?"

Smitty nodded.

"I don't think so," said Nellie. "Why would a man bother to make a note, on a piece of cigarette paper, of his own address? You aren't apt to forget your own address."

"Maybe it wasn't his," said Smitty. "Maybe this shop is owned by someone else, or used by many as a head-quarters. A place for loot, maybe. Anyhow, we'll find out. Then I'll phone police headquarters. We don't want to hold out information on the cops."

"Smitty," said Nellie, with almost a note of exuber-ance in her voice, "I think we're being followed."

"Huh?" said Smitty.

"Yes. The same headlights have been behind us since we left the Coyle Hotel." Her voice was contented. The half-pint blonde lived for excitement.

Smitty began doubling back and forth to shake a possible trailer.

"In that case," said Smitty, carefully, "I'll take you to the chief's place where you'll be safe—"

"You and who else will take me?" blazed Nellie. "What do you think I am—something made out of glass that has to be kept in cotton wool?"

Smitty grinned. He had only been after a rise from her.

The number 87-89 was on a dilapidated-looking building next to a garage on East Eighty-ninth Street. Across the front of the building was the faded sign:

NASH USED-TYPEWRITER CORP.

"I think this is it," said Nellie tensely. "Teebo said it didn't look like an art gallery. This certainly doesn't. How do we get in?"

"How do we usually get in places?" said Smitty.

But the usual way proved all right in this case, as they found when they'd reached the door of the two-story brick building.

Smitty's way was simple.

He put one vast hand on a doorknob and turned it clockwise with about the power of a steam winch. Then he inserted a foot-long piece of pointed steel rod in between the door and the jamb and pried.

This time it wasn't even necessary to use the jimmy. When he turned the knob, there was a thin shriek of breaking metal, a sound like a small bag of gravel being run over; then the lock bar went back and the door opened.

Smitty closed the door carefully and looked out the small, dirty glass panel.

"You must have been wrong about someone's follow-

ing us," he said after a minute. "No car is stopping any-
where near here. Or else we shook them with our doubling around."

"Do you think anyone trailing us would stop right in
front of the building?" sniffed Nellie. "However, I could
have been mistaken."

"First time I ever heard you admit it," grinned Smitty.

Nellie's red lips parted for a stinging rejoinder, but
she didn't make it.

"Let's see if we can find the painting that seems to
have led to Teebo's death," she said.

They found it on the second floor.

The entire first floor of the building was empty. It had
an unused look, too; and Smitty was prepared to bet that
if he inquired he'd find the place was for rent—but that
no amount of money would actually rent it.

The second floor had an equally desolate look, till they
got to the back. There was a small room partitioned off
there, and in this they located a loose floor board. When
the board was pried up they saw a roll of canvas.

Gently, Nellie got it out and unrolled it. In the light
of Smitty's small flash, they looked at it.

Gauguin's "Dock" is one of the major paintings. It
shows a wharf, two small sailing vessels with highly colored sails and several men just getting aboard them. In
the foreground, a small boy, wearing pants too big for
him and a cap too big for him, is looking wistfully at the
sea, longing for the time when he'll be old enough to go,
too.

The boy's face is deeply tanned and his neck and
nose are sun reddened.

"Hasn't he got a red little nose, though?" Nellie exclaimed.

He certainly did have. Gauguin customarily used raw,
strong colors. Here he had outdone himself. The boy's

20

nose was like a little raw tomato from the seaside sun.

Smitty grinned. "That's a trademark, all right. I remember, now. I saw this in Paris once, and I still remember the boy's nose—"

He snapped the flash out. There was no need for Nellie to ask why, because she had heard it, too.

A faint sound of something moving outside the partitioned off space in which they crouched.

Smitty stood up, with Nellie behind him. She glared at him for the care he was taking.

"Don't be a dope," he whispered, lips close to her ear. "We were dancing. Neither of us has on his bulletproof panties and scanties."

Suddenly, there was no attempt at concealment of noise outside.

"They were here, all right," same a cultured voice. "The broken lock proved that. But they must have gone."

"Unless they're in that room," came a voice not so cultured. "We ain't looked in there, yet."

"If so, they'll never snoop around again. There are six of us. And we can use our guns as much as we please. This place means nothing to us."

"O.K., guys. Fan out."

"We must get at the picture," came the cultured voice. "I shall take care of that myself—"

There was a stabbing beam of light from a flash bigger than Smitty's. And then the room was full of men. Smitty and Nellie were flattened against the wall next to the door.

Smitty's idea was simple. They'd steal out while the men were facing forward and while the flashlight rayed that way and left the space in back of it in blackness. And for a minute it looked as if the two would be able to escape like that.

Then the man in the lead exclaimed sharply.

21

"The floor board. Look! It's been pried up!"

At the same time there came a yell from Smitty's right. "They're here! Get 'em!"

That started it.

Six men piled onto the big fellow and the small girl. The men, naturally, split in what seemed a proper ratio—five to handle the giant, one to take the easy job of subduing the girl.

It was an uncomfortable mistake for the one. He didn't know Nellie.

The little blonde looked as if a hard wind would blow her away. She looked as if she'd scream if she saw a mouse. She looked as if one careless slap would knock her unconscious for a week. The fact of the matter was that she was a past mistress of jujitsu, could wrestle and box like a little champion, and was as hard to hold as a basketful of snakes.

The one man tackling her found that out in about a third of a second. He aimed a blow at her face, being not quite all a gentleman should be, and found his fist caught in two small white hands. Then he found himself being propelled forward, half by his own momentum, half by the direction of the amazing little blonde.

After that, he found himself doing a pinwheel through the air which ended with his sliding on chest and chin till the wall brought him up with a bang.

"Hah!" said Nellie. And she turned to the rest.

Smitty's methods were less subtle. When he saw a face, he struck at it. He didn't care if there was a scientific guard blocking the blow or not. If there were, he simply knocked the man out with his own guard, driving the protecting fist back against the jaw behind it with such force that nothing could block the blow. If there wasn't a guard—

There was no guard in the first case. The man was bending to get Smitty around the legs and bring him down. So the big fellow hammered straight down on the top of the fellow's head with a fist like a sledge hammer. He heard a kind of crack and didn't know if it was a neck vertebra or a collar bone. He didn't care much, either.

A clubbed gun glanced from the side of his head. That annoyed him. He whirled, lashing out with a gigantic fist as he did so and caught the clubber on the shoulder. It was a blow that ordinarily wouldn't have amounted to much, but it was Smitty's virtue that he hit so incredibly hard that it didn't matter where his fists landed.

The blow sent this man against the wall so that he fell in a scramble over the man Nellie had sent flying.

And then the fight changed character.

Six to one. This crew must have thought it wasn't necessary to use guns. But they had changed their minds, now, with two out of the fight and a third woozy with slapping the wall.

There was a deliberate shot, and Smitty felt air against his cheek. He roared and plunged. The flashlight went out as its holder crashed to the floor.

But the big fellow had decided it was time to get out of there. As he'd said, they didn't have on their bulletproof underwear, made of the marvelous, steel-strong flexible stuff which The Avenger had invented and called cellu-glass.

"Get a shield," he yelled to Nellie.

She already had one. Another man reaching for her—more cautiously than the first, but still not cautiously enough—had found his arm caught in a grip that made him yell with pain. Nellie's pink and white fingers had found a great nerve center near the elbow where such agony was produced by pressure that the owner would do anything desired.

23

In this case, he was to back to the door with Nellie, shielding her from bullets.

Smitty had a struggling figure held in front of him. The shooting was continuing, bullet after bullet plowing out in darkness. The giant caught the meaning of it.

No one could see where to shoot. But if they kept pumping lead at the doorway, no one could go through it.

Smitty had just figured this out when the figure he held screamed and slumped. A slug had caught the man. There was a cessation of firing. The man with the gun must have thought he'd hit his prey instead of his own man.

In the lull, Smitty and Nellie got out the door. They ran for the stairs.

"After them!" yelled the leader.

Smitty and Nellie raced down the dark stairs, with the thundering feet behind them. But at the foot of the stairs, Nellie drew Smitty toward the back of the place instead of the front.

She had picked the gun from the nerveless fingers of her shield. She threw the gun at the front door. It hit with a bang, as if someone had gone out to the street and slammed the door shut after him.

The men yelled and went out the door, too. There were four still navigating.

"O.K.," said Nellie calmly.

They went to the rear, broke open a window and climbed out to an areaway. But Smitty stopped suddenly.

"The picture!" he said. "We ought to get that. There's so much commotion about it that we ought to take it to the chief. I'll go back for—"

"Don't bother," said Nellie, very calmly indeed. "I have it."

"When in thunder did you get time to pick it up?"

"As I was backing out the door, I felt it with my feet; so I just stooped for it. One hand was enough to control my shield with the nerve pressure."

CHAPTER III

Deadly Interview

Bleek Street in New York is now famous because it has become known that The Avenger has his headquarters there. It wouldn't be famous if it weren't for The Avenger, however. It is only a block long. One side is taken up by the wall of a windowless warehouse. The other side consists of stores and smaller warehouses, all vacant, and a row of three narrow brick buildings in the center.

Dick Benson, The Avenger, has all that side under lease or ownership. In effect, he owns the block.

The three dingy buildings in the center were his headquarters. Behind their grimy façade, they have been thrown into one and are outfitted and furnished as few buildings ever have been.

The top floor was the meeting place for the band, which was known as Justice, Inc. It was there that Benson sat when Smitty and Nellie came in with the painting at a quarter of one in the morning.

27

Volumes have been written about The Avenger. They have all left the enigmatic soul of the man unknown and secret. All that can be described is his physical appearance.

That is unusual enough.

Dick Benson was not a big man, though the legends around his name would lead you to expect a giant even larger than Smitty. On the contrary, The Avenger was about average height and was built with deceptive slimness. But then a steel rod is also slim.

He had hair that was coal-black, close cut, and fitting his head almost like a virile cap. In contrast, his eyes were pale gray, almost colorless, and as cold as ice under a polar moon. His features were really handsome, but you never noticed that. You only noticed that they were so calm, so controlled, that they seemed like a mask.

Dick was alone in the huge top-floor room when Smitty and Nellie came in. They told him what had happened, then unrolled "The Dock." Benson stared at it with ice-clear eyes.

In the daylight luminosity of the special bulbs illuminating the place, the raw colors of the painting fairly leaped at you. It looked as if it had been done with a knife instead of a brush. But it was beautiful.

"This Teebo said he tried to get in touch with me and couldn't?" The Avenger said. His voice was quiet but carried such authority that one's first instinct on hearing it was to jump to obey.

"That's right," replied Nellie.

"He started with you to the place where he kept it, and then disappeared out that window?"

"Yes," said Nellie.

"And you were trailed when you went to the Eighty-ninth Street place?" continued Benson.

"Yes. And the trailers caught up with us there." Nellie bit her lip thoughtfully. "They might have been part of the same gang, partners of Teebo."

"I don't think so," said Smitty. "Remember when we

were trying to hide from that gang? One of them—it sounded like the leader—said they could shoot as much as they pleased; that the place made no difference to them. As if it was the lair of some other gang."

Benson was still staring at the picture.

"On the surface, then," he said, "it looks as if there were two gangs. One, Teebo's, had this picture, and maybe many more, to sell secretly for whatever it would bring. The other gang was trying to highjack the painting, or paintings. In the course of that, they saw Teebo approaching you with the object of selling 'The Dock,' and murdered him to prevent that before they could get their hands on the picture."

"That's the way it looks," said Nellie.

"But looks are sometimes deceiving," Dick mused, his eyes colder than ever as they rested on the painting. "And here is a good example of that. An excellent example. This painting is a fake!"

"A fake?" gasped Smitty.

"Yes. It's only a copy of the real painting. A clever one, but still a copy."

"Then why on earth," said Nellie, "was murder committed for it?"

"I would like to know that, too," said The Avenger, with the cold interest appearing in his eyes that promised bad news to some racketeer, somewhere.

"You're sure of this, chief?" persisted Smitty.

"I'm sure. We'll make a few tests, but I'm sure without them. I remember this picture vividly, and the original was not quite the same in one respect—the boy's nose. Gauguin made it red, but not that red."

If anyone else had talked like this, Smitty and Nellie would have laughed. The idea of remembering every tint in a picture, seen thousands of miles away and years ago, enough to spot a copy as a fake, sounded preposterous.

But they knew the marvelous eye for color Benson

had, and his equally marvelous memory, and they believed. They'd have put the picture down as a fake just on his word, without any of the X-ray tests he proceeded to make.

The tests, though, proved it conclusively. The painting was only a copy, smuggled out of France.

"That settles a point," said Nellie suddenly.

"What?" said Smitty.

"I thought Teebo was a stranger to this country when he talked to us. I'm sure, now. No one knowing anything about American collectors would be ignorant of the kind of man the chief is. And no man in his right mind, knowing about the chief, would dream of trying to sell him a phony painting!"

Smitty nodded agreement. "That brings us back to the first thought—that it was Teebo's own gang that killed him. Maybe one of them saw him pulling the boner of trying to sell a fake to The Avenger, and killed him so the sale wouldn't go through and the racket be discovered."

"Phooey!" said Nellie. "They wouldn't have to kill Teebo to prevent a sale. All they'd have to do would be to tell him to lay off."

Benson said nothing. To the exclusion of everything else, he was staring at the picture. Particularly at the little boy's sun-reddened nose.

Smitty sighed with something like disappointment.

"Anyhow, it begins to look like just another racket— a swell time to smuggle copies of famous paintings into the United States and sell them for fancy prices as originals. So what? The police can handle that without the services of Justice, Inc."

It was just then that the vestibule buzzer sounded.

Nellie stepped to a table on which was a little black box. The box was a miniature television set, a marvel of its kind, designed by Smitty. It showed whoever was in the vestibule downstairs.

The little blonde stared at the person who had rung for admittance at one-thirty in the morning.

"Tall, athletic, fair-haired, well-dressed," she said. "About thirty. Very good-looking," she added.

Smitty snorted. Nellie was always pretending interest in handsome strangers, which burned up the giant.

The Avenger nodded and Nellie pressed the buzzer which opened the door from vestibule to tiny elevator that went only to this top-floor room.

If this sounds careless in a place where giant plans against the underworld are hatched, reckless in men who are so hated by criminals that anyone of a hundred would have given all he had to kill them, remember the character of the place.

The Avenger's headquarters was like a fortress. The elevator was automatically sealed so that a visitor could get off nowhere but on the top floor. There, an electric eye searched him for weapons. Further, there were, in the vast room, half a hundred devices that could be discharged by secret pressures to disable an attacker.

It was unthinkable that anyone should be able to just walk in and do any harm to the place or its occupants. It was so unthinkable that it didn't occur to any of the members of Justice, Inc.

They were about to get a lesson on the possibility of the impossible.

The elevator door slid back with a smooth sound, and their visitor stepped into the room. Nellie watched the recorder of the electric eye. There was no indication of metal in large enough bulk to be a weapon. No hint of dagger or gun. The eye went from the soles of a man's feet to the crown of his head, too. Even a weapon hidden in a shoe or a hat would have been indicated.

"Good evening," said the man. "Are you, sir, Mr. Benson?"

"I am Benson," The Avenger said, his face calm.

"You'll pardon the lateness of the hour," said the man.

31

He looked worried, almost frightened. "But such is the urgency of my business that I could not wait till morning."

Benson merely nodded, icy-pale eyes like beams of light on the handsome, worried face.

"My name is Harris," said the man. "And the business I have to take up with you—concerns that painting! Don't move, any of you!"

He was worried-looking no longer. Instead, desperate triumph was in his eyes. And in his hand was a flat pink flask of colorless but oily-looking liquid that Smitty identified on sight, with a feeling of ice along his spine, as nitroglycerin.

"If any of the three of you moves a muscle," said the man tensely but calmly, "I'll drop this. Needless to describe what a pint of this stuff can do to the building and to us all."

Smitty found himself holding his breath. So was Nellie. The Avenger stood near the table on which was "The Dock," not moving an inch, not even an expression on his face.

"I am aware," said the man composedly, "that you have many trick inventions in here. But please remember that no one of them could overpower me quickly enough to prevent me from dropping this nitroglycerin. In fact, even if I were struck instantly dead, in my falling would come your destruction."

Smitty stared with fascination at Dick's calmness. They were in the deadliest danger of their lives. There was no doubt of that. Each of them knew surely that this man was not bluffing. They did as he wanted, or they died!

But the expressionlessness of The Avenger's face persisted. He seemed so unmoved, indeed, that the man who called himself Harris was urged to cold anger.

"If you think I won't do it—" he began.

"I am quite sure you would," said Benson evenly. "What do you want us to do?"

"I want you to stay right where you are, moving neither feet nor hands, while I walk out with that painting," said the man.

"Aren't you taking desperate risks just to get hold of a fake?" The Avenger suggested.

"A fake?" Harris repeated. He was quite indifferent about it. "Is it, really?"

"It is only a worthless copy."

"Regardless," said Harris, "I'll have it. Don't move!"

He came calmly toward The Avenger, passing within easy reach of the trained hands, slim and not strong-looking but which were like chilled steel in their incredible strength.

And Benson didn't reach with those hands.

Harris picked up the painting and backed toward the door. Not the elevator door, because he could be trapped in that tiny cage and knew it. He went toward the door leading to a stairway, which could not be entered from below but could be used as an exit by anyone inside, due to a system of intricate one-way locks.

In the doorway, the man paused. There was still triumph on his face but there was no gloating there. He was not only a brave man, he was an intelligent one. He knew that while he had beaten The Avenger, that did not mean that Benson wasn't a dangerous antagonist.

"You might trap me on the stairs," he said, "but even there, if I dropped this flask, the whole building would go down, burying you in it. I leave it to you to decide whether the loss of a fake painting is worth that."

He turned, and Smitty looked at Nellie, angry and undecided and astounded. That someone should walk in here—here—and be able to pick up an object and walk out again in defiance of them all was simply unbelievable.

"Hey! Nobody can do that to us!" groaned the giant.

"It seems that it is being done," said Dick Benson evenly.

"We've got to stop him!"

"Go ahead," said Nellie. "The job's all yours." And she shivered as she remembered the TNT—enough to blow them all sky-high.

Meanwhile, they heard the steady sound of Harris' feet descending the stairs.

The Avenger went to his huge desk and sat down. He seemed almost indifferent.

"The electric indicator gave no warning," he said, "because the man's weapon was of glass instead of metal. We must remedy that defect so that this cannot happen again."

They distinctly heard the outer door, three floors down, open and close.

"Chief, he's getting away!" wailed Nellie.

The pale, icy eyes were expressionless.

"Let him go," Benson said. "Why not? The painting is without value. And we have had a chance to examine it for any significant peculiarities."

Smitty and Nellie hadn't thought of that. After all, there was no reason to fight and bleed and die for something worthless.

But then Nellie had a thought.

"Say! That picture wasn't worth anything as a picture —but maybe it had some important message on it. Under the paint, for example."

"You forget that we X-rayed it. No message of any kind was revealed," said The Avenger.

The ice-pale eyes were intent in thought.

"That was a brave man," he mused. "And a desperate man. So desperate that he would have blown himself to pieces along with us rather than fail in his mission. Yet, he knew the picture was valueless; he showed no surprise when I told him. One thing is certain. No criminal would risk his life like that even for a genuine painting worth a hundred thousand dollars. That means that whatever this picture business may be, it is not an ordinary racket."

"But that only means that, somehow, the thing has great importance," mourned Smitty. "And we had to let him get away!"

For an instant something that might almost have been a smile touched the corners of Dick Benson's lips.

"Stand where I was standing, at that table on which the picture rested," he said to Smitty.

Wondering, the giant took his place there.

"Now, look behind you."

Smitty looked and exclaimed aloud. He had forgotten something that rested behind that table; and it was odd that he should have forgotten it was because he was its inventor.

There was a cabinet there, and the front of the cabinet was a screen over which soft fluorescence played constantly, though it was almost unnoticeable in the brilliant illumination of the daylight bulbs. The cabinet was the container of the last word in television sets, as far beyond the standard commercial sets as they, in turn, are beyond the old crystal sets.

The power was on and had been on all during the deadly interview. And most of the action had taken place where the transmitter would catch it all.

"I signaled Mac's drugstore with my toe against the floor switch when Harris drew out the flask," Benson said. "Someone must be following him, now."

CHAPTER IV

Apology for Murder

At first glance the store seemed just what it appeared to be—an ordinary drugstore. And so it was, in front. But the rear room, which was twice as big as the store part and which was partitioned off in steel, was not at all what you'd have expected to find in the back of a drugstore.

It was a huge dual laboratory. One side was taken up with electrical and radio apparatus, and it was here that Smitty conducted his experiments.

The other half was for chemical experiments. Here worked the proprietor of the store, Fergus MacMurdie.

MacMurdie had been about to close up the shop when the signal came for him to stand by for a television message from the Bleek Street headquarters.

Benson was the one who had set Mac up in this store. Benson was Mac's chief, whose orders he obeyed instantly and without question. Mac would have died for Dick Benson.

37

So he almost dropped a vial of concentrated sulphuric on his toes in his haste to get to the screen when the signal light glowed.

Mac was tall and bony and had bleak blue eyes. His hair was coarse and reddish and so was his skin. He had ears that stood out from his head like sails, and a pair of the biggest feet in captivity. But no one ever laughed at Mac. Not twice, anyway.

His dour blue eyes took in about five seconds of the tableau on the television screen, and then he yelled: "Cole! Cole Wilson!"

Cole was the newest member of Justice, Inc. He was magnetic, husky, with wavy dark hair and romantic eyes. He was almost too good-looking; but his friends paid no attention to his good looks because they knew that he was a devil on wheels in any fight.

Cole was in the front of the store. Something in Mac's voice told him there'd be no more routine business that night. He jumped to the store door and locked it, then clicked off the lights. No customers were in the store. This would keep any would-be customers out.

He raced back to the rear room to find Mac standing, fascinated, at the television screen. So Cole stared, too, and he heard and saw most of what had gone on at Bleek Street.

"My gosh!" he kept breathing as the play unrolled. "With a whiskey bottle full of nitro, this guy walks right in, and I guess he's going to walk right out again with the picture. Look at the chief's right hand!"

Both saw it—the little move of the thumb and third finger of Benson's right hand. That was a code signal meaning: "Follow this man."

The signal was hardly necessary. As Cole stared, he was reaching for his belt radio, the tiny two-way set of Smitty's perfecting that allowed each member of the band to communicate with others no matter where they were.

38

He fastened the thin, curved case under his shirt at the belt.

" 'Tis the picturrre," burred Scotch MacMurdie. "That's what he came for—"

"Of course," said Cole impatiently. He didn't know what this was about, where the chief had gotten a rolled-up canvas or what it meant; but he needed no one to point out that the picture was the reason for the invasion of Bleek Street.

Cole was on his way before the man paused in the stair doorway at Justice, Inc., with the flask menacingly raised. He reached the mouth of Bleek Street just as a car roared away from the curb.

Cole had just time to see that there was only one man in the car, the driver, and that he was a blond fellow. Then he whirled off after the man in his own car.

The car Cole was driving was a deceptive affair. The Avenger himself used it often, because its disguise was so good. It was a moderately priced, large sedan, about four years old. It was shabby and sedate. But under the weathered hood was a motor that would whirl the chassis along at over a hundred miles an hour.

It was lucky that Cole had such speed. He found out that he was going to need it.

The driver of the car ahead was in a hurry that took no account of laws. He went sixty miles an hour up Sixth Avenue and fifty across town to the elevated highway. Three times, he swung up over curbs and down sidewalks for a few yards to get through traffic jams taking up the whole street.

Cole swerved with him.

They reached the West Side Highway going north, and at this point the man ahead pushed it up to seventy-five. Cole dropped behind. He reflected resentfully that you never saw a traffic cop if you needed one. It would be a help if a motorcycle cop appeared and pinched this guy.

But then he remembered the hour, the one time in the twenty-four hours that a car had a slight chance of speeding like this and not being caught.

Cole kept on dropping behind. Till now, he'd had no chance to try to conceal the fact that he was pursuing the fellow ahead. Now, he tried to lull the man's suspicions, if there were any to lull.

He began to think there were none. It seemed as if any man in such a frantic hurry to get away must have noticed the car hugging his tail. But this man acted as if unconscious of pursuit.

Or as if sure that at any time he could rid himself of such pursuit!

"I wonder," said Cole Wilson, reflecting apprehensively along this line, "if he has got something that could stop me."

A bomb, at least of the pineapple size commonly carried by crooks, wouldn't do it. The old sedan was armored like a tank. Shots wouldn't do it; the car was bulletproof. Then what?

Cole shrugged. He decided that nothing could shake his pursuit. He sped on in the wake of the other man, and now found he was doing eighty.

They went farther and farther uptown. Then they went around a traffic circle and down a small road. And there Cole found out the reason why the man ahead seemed so little bothered by a trailer.

His car approached a fork where five roads came together in a bewildering mess. There was no other car in sight. The man shot toward this many-pronged fork, and there was a sharp puff of sound from his car. Also, there was a cloud of black smoke.

He had raised a smoke screen, exactly as a destroyer at sea raises a smoke screen to hide itself or a battle ship. And he was being just as successful.

"Hey!" exclaimed Cole.

There had been a car. Now, there was a black cloud hiding the beginning of all the five roads.

"Jeu!"

There was no way on earth of telling which of the five roads his quarry had taken. This was why he had driven so confidently.

Cole slammed on his brakes, but such was his speed that he couldn't stop till he was into the cloud. There, he stopped, all right. He hit a curb, glanced off and nuzzled to rest against a tree. He couldn't see a thing, blinded in that smoke.

"I've muffed him," he mourned disconsolately.

He rolled down the right-hand window to find out if he could see a little better with no glass between him and the smoke. He couldn't. He got out. In a moment the smoke would clear; then he could see where he was in relation to the road and perhaps find out into which lane the other car had turned.

It was three or four minutes before he could see anything even dimly. Then, so close at hand that he almost jumped, he saw the other car!

It hadn't taken any road at all. It had stopped right after throwing the smoke screen. Why? Well, Cole was to find that out in about a second.

He started impulsively toward the car, balling his fist to give the driver a good, persuasive clout!

Cole Wilson was a ball of fire in action. There was no member of Justice, Inc., who had performed more marvels than he had. But he had one fault.

He was impulsive.

Any other of the little band would have thought it out a minute before leaping toward the car. But not Cole. So he got into trouble.

"Stand perfectly still, please," came a voice.

He whirled. Coming around the side of his own car was the man he was after.

41

The smoke had been, not an escape effort, but an attempt to lure him out of his own machine where he was accessible to trouble. And the attempt had succeeded.

"Turn around," said the man.

He had an automatic that looked like a cannon. He was almost courteous, but there was impersonal murder in his tone.

Cole hesitated. There was still much smoke, but there was not too much murk for the man to drill him in the head quite easily if he wanted to.

Cole turned.

He knew the trick, of course. The man would prefer not to shoot if he didn't have to. Better to club him down silently. So he was going to walk up behind Cole's back, and slash the automatic down.

If Cole could spot the precise instant when the gun was upraised, and hence off line, he'd try a break.

He felt, rather than heard, the man's cautious steps over the turf behind him. He thought he heard a rustle of fabric as the man's arm raised, but he wasn't sure. Not sure enough.

Sweat burst out on his forehead. It was a deadly guessing game. If he guessed wrong, he had his skull smashed, for he knew this fellow would play for keeps. If he guessed right—

He whirled and sprang. And the luck of The Avenger's aides was with him. The gun was swung up for the blow.

Frantically, the man tried to get it down for a shot, but he was at least a half second too late. Then he grunted as a fist caught him in the middle and another tagged his jaw. Hard fingers tore the gun from his grasp, but he was at least able to twitch it away so Wilson couldn't get it. It fell in the dark. Then it was man to man.

The fight that followed was a honey.

Cole was as fast as light, as tough as whipcord, and was now pretty sore. He would rather not go back to Bleek Street at all than go without the man he'd been sent for, and he fought with that grim thought in mind.

The blond fellow fought as though death were better than defeat. And as far as strength and swiftness went, he, too, was quite a battler.

He straightened from that first blow, and caught Cole over the heart with a right that made The Avenger's man feel as if he'd been stabbed. Then he got one in on the side of Cole's face that made him see stars.

Cole came back with a double jab to the middle again, and a short one straight up to the jaw. The man reeled backward. Cole followed, then felt a hand suddenly seize on his face, with fingers jabbing viciously for his eyes.

He had to back off or go blind. And as he backed, his opponent jumped like a tiger, caught him squarely around the waist and laid him on the ground like a falling tree. His hands went around Cole's windpipe.

Cole wrenched at the iron fingers. He seemed to hear far-off bells ringing. Also, he seemed to hear something that acted on his flagging strength like a shot of adrenalin.

He seemed to hear men running toward them through the clearing, black smoke. Many men.

Cole stopped clawing at the throttling hands. He bent his arm back to get the last possible inch of distance for the blow and punched up at the man's face. It was a ten-inch jab that a champion might have been proud of. It rocked the fellow's head far back.

Wilson followed it with a second, felt the choking hands relax and threw the man off. One last punch ended in a sort of cracking sound. And it was Cole who delivered it.

He saw the blond guy fall limply. But now he heard the running steps close by. Without pause, he leaped for the man's car. On the front seat was the rolled-up canvas. He snatched it and went back to his unconscious attacker.

"Harris," a voice rumbled almost at his elbow. "Where are you? This damned smoke—"

Wilson picked up the man and sped with him to his

43

own old sedan. He jammed the unconscious body into the right-hand side, then ran around to the driver's seat.

They saw him, then. And he saw them. There were a dozen of them. More. Twenty at least, most with guns in their hands.

"It's a young army," rasped Cole. "What is all this?"

But it didn't matter what it was. He had won. With exuberance in his grin and triumph in his pumping blood, he slammed the door shut and started the motor. Now to go back to Bleek Street with both man and painting—

One whiplike revolver shot robbed him of most of his victory!

Almost as it came, Cole suddenly remembered that the window on the unconscious man's side was open. He had rolled it down to try to see through the smoke. He whipped across to roll up the bulletproof glass; but then the shot had come!

Cole cursed as he saw the blond fellow's head jerk and saw that a bullet had drilled it squarely. Then he was ducking as more shots poured at the raising window. He got it up, and, after that, they could shoot all they pleased. But they'd got his prisoner first.

Soon, they saw that their shots were wasted, and they stopped firing. As mysteriously as they had appeared, they faded back into the night, and Cole was helpless to stop them.

He cursed some more on his way back to Bleek Street with the dead man. With no inkling of what the chief had headed him into, Cole sensed that Benson would have given a lot to have this man alive in order to question him.

There'd be no questions answered now. And that fact, though of course no one of Justice, Inc., could guess that, was to result in tragedy.

But Cole Wilson had another thing to gnaw at his angry brain as he drove back to Manhattan and to Bleek

44

Street. That was something he thought he had heard just before the shot had finished off his prisoner.

In fact, he was sure he had heard it.

Quite distinctly, he had heard the marksman say, "Sorry, my friend."

Then the fatal shot.

It was almost as if the man had, incredibly, been apologizing for murder. But then the man himself had been rather incredible, too. Cole had seen him quite clearly.

He was a monstrously fat man. He must have weighed nearly three hundred pounds.

CHAPTER V

The Devil's Yardstick

The morning sun poured in through the steel slats that protected the windows of the Bleek Street headquarters from bullets. It had been a hectic night, climaxed by Cole Wilson's chase after the blond man who had called himself Harris.

They were all in the vast top-floor room now, talking over the affair of the fake painting. By now, it was crystal clear that something tremendous lay behind it.

On The Avenger's desk were objects from the dead man's pockets. The man himself now lay on a slab at the morgue, after an examination of his person that told nothing at all.

Nellie, Smitty, MacMurdie and Wilson all stared at one thing above all that had come from the man's clothes.

This, at first glance, seemed to be a folding ruler. But if so, it was calibrated as no ruler ever was. It didn't have inches marked on it. It didn't have anything marked on it but lines. That was all right; some rulers have the inches marked off but the figures omitted. However, these lines didn't represent inches. They were spread all over the place.

Benson had measured them a moment ago. There were five lines marked on the ruler. The first was an inch and seven eighths from the end; the second, three inches; the third, five and a half; the fourth, nine and a quarter inches; the fifth, and last, fourteen and three quarters. There was also a single mark on the other side.

What possible sense could be made out of that?

Furthermore, very faintly, there were traces of many previous markings, which had been rubbed out when new ones were added. It was as if this ruler had been used many times to measure many queer distances.

"Cole," said The Avenger, his voice calm but full of that command which made him a born leader of men, "you are sure you heard the killer apologize before he shot?"

"Dead sure," said Cole. "He said, 'Sorry, my friend,' and then he let him have it." He ran his hand through his thick dark hair. "He'd have let me have the slug instead, of course, but he was standing at an angle where he could get the man but not me."

"So he killed his own friend and co-worker, rather than risk having him taken prisoner and made to talk," mused Dick Benson.

"That's what it looks like, chief." Cole, in his anxiety to give every detail that might be helpful, brought one up now that he hadn't thought of before. "The guy was very fat."

Smitty and Nellie whirled on him in unison.

"He was what?"

"I said he was very fat. The killer, I mean," Cole repeated, looking surprised at their consternation. "He must have weighed nearly three hundred pounds. His face was heavy-jowled, and he looked like the kind of fellow who'd need a shave an hour after he had one."

Smitty stared at Nellie, who slowly shook her head.

"I know what you're thinking, and it simply can't be."

"That's the exact description of Teebo," said Smitty stubbornly.

"Teebo jumped forty-four stories to hard sidewalk," said Nellie. "Don't be dumb."

"I know. Teebo's dead. We saw his . . . er . . . what was left of him. Just the same, this guy that Cole describes sounds like Teebo."

"Look, you mountain of ignorance, the dead don't walk! Particularly when they've been mashed as flat as a—"

The Avenger spoke suddenly. As usual, his concentration on the problem at hand was so intense that he had heard nothing irrelevant to the job.

"If there's one thing certain by now," he said, "it is that this is not an ordinary fake-masterpiece racket."

"Teebo acted as if it were," retorted Nellie. "He acted as if his sole business was to sell a phony for as much money as he could get for it."

"I believe Teebo thought that was all there was to it," Dick agreed. "Perhaps he had associates who believed the same way; that it was only a racket. Honest crooks, you might call them."

"Then where does the man fit in who came here for the painting?" asked Smitty.

"I don't know," said Benson.

"And the gang I ran into at the five corners, one of whom shot the blond guy?" said Cole.

The Avenger shook his head. "I don't know their place in this, either. But the fact that Teebo was murdered to prevent the sale of the fake Gauguin to me indicates that there are two separate gangs. As Nellie pointed out, members of Teebo's own gang wouldn't have had to kill him to prevent the sale of a fake to an organization they knew was dangerous to them. All they'd have had to do was tip

49

Teebo off to leave the Pink Room without seeing Smitty or Nellie again."

"Was Teebo murdered?" Smitty murmured, looking at the ceiling. "This fat man Cole described—"

"Has nothing to do with Teebo," Nellie finished with a snap. "Dry up, will you? There are lots of fat men."

Under Mac's dour blue eyes, they both shut up. Cole's gaze went back to the strangely calibrated ruler.

"What do you suppose that is?" he asked Benson.

"I'm afraid the answer is the same as to the other questions," said Benson. "I don't know."

"All we know, then, is that something big is in the wind that has to do with fake paintings. And the death of the man Cole captured leaves us absolutely without a lead."

"That's right," said The Avenger. "So we will make a lead."

They looked inquiringly at him.

"Almost certainly, Teebo's crowd has sold, or tried to sell, other phony masterpieces to other wealthy collectors," Dick said. "We'll check and find out. One of the wealthiest and best-known in New York is Clay Marsden. Cole, you might pay Marsden a visit. See if he has recently bought a famous European picture and find out if he has had any trouble since the purchase."

Cole's thought showed on his good-looking face, and The Avenger answered it without Cole's having to speak.

"Yes, I know it will be difficult to get a man to admit that he has bought stolen goods, which is what any masterpiece from Europe would be today. I'll leave it to your ingenuity to ferret out the information. Meanwhile, we may short-cut the personal-investigation method on other collectors."

His steely forefinger pressed a button on his desk. The stair door of the big top-floor room opened, and Josh and Rosabel Newton came in from their second-floor apartment.

Josh was a Negro, gangling, stooped, with feet even bigger than MacMurdie's, and with a look of being about to go to sleep on his feet. Actually, he was an honor graduate of Tuskegee Institute with a brain like a steel trap, and could fight like a black panther in an emergency.

Rosabel, his wife, was quite pretty. The two were caretakers of Justice, Inc., in peaceful times, and doughty fighters when trouble came.

"Josh," said Dick, "I want you and Rosabel to go over the news reports of the last six months. Note any disturbance, particularly burglary or assault, that may have happened in connection with any person known to be a collector of famous paintings."

"Yes, sir," said the Negro. "Anything else?"

"Yes. One other thing. Every time you find such an incident, look over the general news in that same time period and see if you find any curious coincidences."

"You mean," asked Rosabel, "that a collector may have something happen to him and, following that, there may be an apparently unrelated crime, like a murder? Another collector is attacked, and a little later perhaps there's another and similar murder?"

"That's the stuff," said Benson. "Search for news events that may possibly be similar in character after raids on collectors."

"Right," said Josh.

The two left, to go down to the first floor.

Benson had a news teletype in his headquarters which gave constant ticker tape reports on all news. The tapes were filed in chronological order on the first floor. The Avenger had given Josh and Rosabel a complicated and lengthy task, but he knew they'd come up with something—if there was anything to come up with.

CHAPTER VI

Loot of War

As in this affair of the fake Gauguin, it was Dick Benson's practice to make a lead when no natural ones developed.

In this case, after he had set Josh and Rosabel onto past news and sent Cole Wilson to the Marsden home, a natural lead occurred.

The Avenger was once more checking the painting. He was making sure, once again, that there was no message under the oils—nothing in either visible or invisible ink, printed on the canvas before that canvas was covered with paint by the clever copyist who had reproduced "The Dock."

There was no such message. That was positive.

His pale eyes had gone over the composition of the painting. Could the grouping of subjects, or the arrangement of lines, have presented a message? Or a map or something?

But this wasn't probable, either. Gauguin had painted

a picture just to be painting a picture. It would be impossible to distort a copy into spelling out some message without so altering the lines that a glance would tell that it wasn't an original.

Nellie was at the news ticker, watching the unreeling tape.

"We're sure on a hot trail, chief," said the little blonde. "About seeing if other collectors have had some kind of troubles. Listen to this:

" 'Durban Vaughan, well-known artists' agent and owner of the Manhattan Art Gallery, has just been reported murdered. His body was found in his office at 2 P.M. by an employee returning from a late lunch. Police are now investigating.' "

"We'll join them in the investigation," Dick said. "Mac!"

The two went out—the tall Scot with the dour blue eyes and the lithe, chilled-steel bar of a man called The Avenger.

"Leaving me to rot here doing nothing," Nellie said resentfully to Smitty.

"Leaving both of us," mourned the giant. "I can't understand it in my case. In yours, I can. The chief is on important business. It wouldn't help any to have you go and get in a jam so that a couple of us had to drop the main job and go to your rescue—"

He ducked just in time to keep an angrily flung book from bouncing off his head.

It didn't look as if they were going to miss any excitement, however. Benson and Mac were simply on a routine murder investigation.

At least that was what it started out to be.

The Manhattan Gallery is on upper Fifth Avenue. Crowds stream past all day, and there are usually several people in the gallery. It is about the last place anyone would choose for a daylight murder; but murder had been done, nevertheless. And just a glance at the locale told how it could have been committed with no one the wiser.

Durban Vaughan's private office was a full room away from the front, display part. Dick and Mac passed through a storeroom where scores of canvases were stacked and opened a door to the office.

The first thing The Avenger saw was that the door was half a foot thick, like the door of an ice box. That gave him the idea, which only a glance at the walls was needed to confirm, that the office was elaborately soundproof.

This is excellent for comfortable and silent working. But it can—and in this case it had—become a decided disadvantage. No sounds can get in from outside to disturb concentration. But no sounds can get outside, either, even the sound of yells, to attract attention.

And in the death of Durban Vaughan, there must have been yells!

The man, middle-aged, partly bald, a little too heavy, lay in front of the door of his office vault. His shoes and socks were off, and there were burns on his feet.

A lieutenant of detectives named Parsons was in charge of the case. Parsons had met The Avenger several times.

"Hello, Mr. Benson," he said. "I'm glad you're interesting yourself in this case. It looks like a tough one. No one saw anybody come in here; no one knows what they were after. It's a blind alley."

"You have found nothing important?" said Benson, pale eyes ranging the big private office.

"Nothing," said Parsons.

"You have no idea what the killers were torturing this man to get?"

"No, sir." Parsons was over fifty. The Avenger was in his twenties. But that "sir" just naturally slipped out.

"Anything missing?"

"Not as far as we can tell. Or as the clerk who found Mr. Vaughan can tell."

Benson's gaze went to the vault and stayed there.

"It is probably," he said, "that the murderers were torturing Vaughan to make him open that vault. There seems to be nothing else around that they couldn't have searched without his help. I see the vault is now closed. Was it closed when you got here?"

"Yes, sir. I don't think it had ever been opened. You see, Vaughan died of shock caused by the torture. That's what the medical examiner said. There was nothing to kill him, but he died from fright and pain. His heart couldn't stand it—which makes it just as much murder as if he'd been shot."

"Of course," nodded Benson. And though his voice was quite even and calm, Parsons almost shivered when he looked into the pale, glacial eyes.

Benson had seen many cruel things in his work of avenging cruelty, but he could still be profoundly, icily enraged at such things.

"Have you gone over Vaughan's record of purchases yet?" he asked.

Parsons nodded. "His regular ones, anyway. But his senior clerk thinks there have been purchases lately that aren't entered in the books. Private stuff, maybe." The lieutenant looked speculatively at The Avenger. "Such private records, and maybe more stuff we want to see, may be in that vault. Can you open it?"

"I think so," said Benson.

He went to it.

"Have you photographed for fingerprints?" he asked.

"Yes," said Parsons. "Go right ahead. You won't disturb anything."

The Avenger's fingers touched the combination knob of the vault. As strong as tool steel, those fingers were; as sensitive as the strings of a violin; as clever as if each fingertip held a tiny brain.

In about three minutes the vault door swung back.

The lieutenant shook his head. "I'm glad you work

with the cops instead of against them," he said. "Do you want to look around a little before we plow things up?"

"I would like to. Thanks."

The Avenger found the little brown book almost at once. It was the main thing he had wanted to see. It recorded transactions in pictures which, for some reason, Vaughan did not want to keep in his regular books.

The last such transaction told why the secrecy was desired. The last entry read:

Dubois' "Diabolo" _____ $94,500.00

The Avenger's almost colorless eyes glinted like ice. The painting, "Diabolo," by Dubois, had been in the Louvre in Paris, last he had heard of it. It was owned by the French government. If Vaughan had bought it here in New York, it was stolen property, looted from the museum during the war disturbance and smuggled into this country. No wonder its purchase was in a private-account book.

In the vault, along with office and gallery records, were a dozen paintings which were obviously too valuable to leave in the regular storeroom. Each was a masterpiece, worth many thousands of dollars.

But Dubois' "Diabolo" was not among them!

"You're sure the killers hadn't gotten into this vault?" Benson asked.

"I can't be sure, of course," Parsons said slowly. "But I am almost sure. You see, there were a lot of prints on the combination knob. But none of them belonged to Vaughan. And his prints would have almost had to be there if the vault had been opened. Not many could walk in here, strange, like you, and open it up."

"You have a theory, then?"

"Yes. As far as it goes. I think several men walked in here off the street—there was only one clerk in the place

57

because it was lunch time—came into this office by surprise and shut and locked the soundproof door before Vaughan could yell for help. I think they wanted something that they were sure was in the vault. So they set about making Vaughan open it. Vaughan took a lot of torture without breaking. Then he up and died of shock on them. They went away without having found what they came for."

"It sounds likely," Dick said.

Parsons grinned with the commendation. This would be something to tell the boys about for a long time.

"Could I see the clerk who found Vaughan's body?" Benson asked.

Parsons called him.

His name was Wendell, and he looked like a tired professor. He was Vaughan's senior clerk and had been here for thirty years. He was a little pale, now, as he wondered what would happen to him. Such jobs as his are not plentiful. Where would he get another?

At least, that seemed to be all that bothered him. He certainly didn't act like a guilty man.

"You didn't see anyone go into the office?" Benson asked Wendell.

"No, sir." Wendell paused, then added: "I was quite busy with two important patrons. It would be easy for anyone to pass from street door to back room unseen, while we were discussing pictures in one of the small alcoves."

"Mr. Vaughan's private-account book indicates that he recently bought the 'Diabolo,' by Dubois. Have you seen it?"

"'Diabolo!'" Wendell exclaimed, aghast. "How on earth could anyone get hold of— No, sir, I haven't seen it here. And I didn't know of its purchase, though I've had an idea for several days that Mr. Vaughan got hold of something exciting. It has showed in his manner. Quite buoyant, he has been."

The Avenger's eyes were like steel drills. This struck him as important.

"Since when has his manner been excited, buoyant?"

"Since Monday, four days ago," said Wendell.

"Can you remember any incident that might have been responsible for his elated manner?"

"I'm not sure." Wendell's hand caressed his long, thin jaw. "It seems to me, though, that it began right after a strange fat man came in here to see him."

"A fat man?" snapped Benson.

"Oh, very fat. I think he weighed around three hundred pounds. He had a very heavy beard. The kind that needs shaving twice as often as an ordinary growth. I think his name was Timbu, or Tarbo, or some such—"

"Was it Teebo?"

"Yes, that was it."

Benson and MacMurdie left the shop. Mac looked questioningly at The Avenger.

"Vaughan bought the 'Diabolo,' all right, from Teebo. But it isn't on these premises. I'd like a look at that, to see if it, too, is a fake."

"Maybe he put it in his safe-deposit box," said the canny Scot. "Some of those boxes are as big as trunks. One would take the 'Diabolo,' if 'twas rolled up like 'The Dock.'"

"I don't think he'd choose a bank box as a hiding place," Benson said. "He has a home in Connecticut, I happen to know. The picture may be concealed there, or it may be in his New York apartment. He has a penthouse on Seventy-fourth Street."

He went to the nearest phone booth and called Bleek Street.

"Nellie? Locate the Connecticut home of Durban Vaughan. Go there with Smitty and see if you can find

59

the picture by Dubois called 'Diabolo.' It will probably be well hidden."

"Right, chief," came the little blonde's clear voice through the receiver.

Dick turned from the phone to MacMurdie.

"We'll take the penthouse, Mac. Come along."

CHAPTER VII

Beautiful Menace

Meanwhile, Cole Wilson had reached the Long Island mansion of Clay Marsden, retired oil magnate and purchaser of museum pieces of art.

The Marsden house was big but not especially elaborate when you remembered all the millions of dollars Marsden was supposed to own. It was set in a half block of lawn, with thick shrubbery. There was a high iron fence and a gate.

The gate was closed. Cole got out of his car and went to it. There was a buzzer in the stone pillar to the right. He pressed this and heard a click. He tried the gate, found it open and walked into the place.

The path led among well-kept bushes and cone-shaped evergreens. All beautiful enough. But Cole was like a trained soldier who does not look at landscape for beauty but for possible ambushes. He looked around here, and he didn't like what he saw.

A dozen men could be hidden, even in daylight, in the

thick clumps of shrubbery. Another dozen could keep the boles of thick trees between them and him. And the house itself, under shade of more trees, loomed dark and somehow mysterious. Its walls were thick—so thick that Cole's first thought was how easy it would be to shoot a man and never have the shot heard outside.

"I'm getting jumpy," Cole reproved himself.

After all, this was just an ordinary mansion, housing ordinary people. It didn't shelter a gang of cutthroats, not here on respectable Long Island.

He felt better after he had reached the big front door with no hint of anyone else on the grounds. He pressed the bell and felt still better when the door was opened. Also, he felt a pleasant tingle of visual satisfaction.

For the door was opened by a girl that any man would look at twice—or five times if possible—on the street.

She was tall, slim but full-curved, with chestnut-brown hair that looked warm enough to kindle a fire, and with light-brown eyes.

She looked pleasant, too. "Yes?" she said. "What is it you want?"

"I'd like to speak to Mr. Marsden, please," Cole told her. He had no hat to take off because he always went bareheaded. But there was a suggestion of a doffed hat in his chivalrous tone. He found himself wishing that he could rescue this girl from some kind of trouble.

"What do you wish to speak to him about?" The girl smiled. "I am Jessica, Mr. Marsden's daughter. You could confide in me."

"I would love to confide almost anything in you," Cole said. "But this particular matter must be confided to your father. If you don't mind—"

"Just step in here," said the girl, smiling. "You can wait in the front hall while I see if he can see you."

Cole went in. Smiling, the girl shut the door. Cole heard the clack of a heavy automatic bolt.

"That's a beautiful Corot," said Cole, staring at a famous picture on the wall. "Is it an original—"

He stopped. He still stared at the picture but, now, without seeing it. He didn't move a finger.

This was because he knew that the thing pressing coldly against the back of his neck was a gun!

"Don't try anything," said the smiling girl it had been such a pleasure to meet, "or I'll blow your head right off."

To say that Cole was amazed at the pressure of that gun in his neck would have been a magnificent understatement. He was not only amazed, he was completely burned to a crisp. Here he had come to this place in the kindliest spirit, to see if anything had happened to Marsden and to offer his help if something had occurred, and he was met with the point of a gun.

"All right," he snapped angrily, "what am I supposed to do now?"

"You're supposed to keep a civil tongue in your head, for one thing," Jessica Marsden snapped back. That reddish-brown hair indicated a temper.

"Would you kindly tell me, please," Cole retorted sarcastically, "what is the big idea, if you don't mind?"

"The idea is that Dad and I are sick of all this. Your gang has tried to break in here; they have tried to bribe our servants to let them in, till finally we had to dismiss the servants. They have tried to kidnap me and kidnap Dad. We're not going to stand it any more."

Cole instantly lost his anger, and became intensely alert. So something hot was going on here at the Marsden home! For the thousandth time, Cole marveled at the way The Avenger could smell out trouble.

He considered telling who he was and asking particulars. Then he had the second thought that if he didn't identify himself, if he let the girl keep on thinking he was a crook, he might learn more from her.

Sober thought might have hinted that this was a foolish

thing to do, but it seemed like a good idea at the time.

"I'm not part of any gang," he protested. But he managed to look as guilty as a captured pickpocket as he said it.

"Oh, no?" Jessica could be sarcastic, too. Her slim right hand went lightly over Cole's shoulders and sides. She came up with a pet weapon of his—a compressed air gun that would shoot a .22 pellet in which was some anaesthetic of MacMurdie's invention. It could snap one of the pellets accurately up to eighty feet, there to crash the glass globule and release a gas that put a victim to sleep almost immediately.

"I suppose you came here to sell us a vacuum cleaner," said Jessica, hefting the gun. "I suppose you get your signatures on the dotted line by the use of a revolver."

"That's not a real gun," said Cole. "Here, I'll show you how it works—"

"Keep your hands still!" Cole was abruptly silent as he felt the steel prod deeper into his neck. "Come on. We'll go and see Dad. You wanted to see him, didn't you?"

"Well—" mumbled Cole, still keeping up the guilty act.

He was marched to the stairs, up them and to a front bedroom. There he was confronted by a middle-aged man in a dressing gown who didn't look well.

"Jess!" the man said. His similarity of features told that he was Marsden, her father. "What in the world—"

"Another of them, Dad," said the girl bitterly. "So I thought we'd entertain this one. Show him real hospitality."

Marsden's dark eyes turned coldly on Cole. "You'll never get it," he said. "You understand? You and your band of cutthroats might as well understand that right now."

"Get what?" fished Cole, keeping up the play by looking sullen.

"I think you know. 'The Princess.' Even if your gang overpowered my daughter and me and had this house to yourselves, you wouldn't get it."

Now Cole was arriving somewhere. So Marsden had bought a masterpiece, too. And he had been bothered after the purchase. Also, the painting—Cole had an idea that it might be Veriner's portrait of the Russian Katrina, now known simply as Veriner's "Princess"—was not in this house. Marsden had told him in so many words that it was concealed elsewhere.

Jessica seemed to realize that slip, too. She looked at her father sideways and said, "Careful, Dad."

Marsden bit his lip. Then he looked inquiringly at his daughter. "Now that you have this bandit, what do you intend to do with him?"

"Keep him here," said the girl.

"Keep him?"

"Yes. Here's our position: We can't go to the police about these attempted burglaries. We can't shut ourselves in this house forever. So we'll keep this man as hostage. If anything happens to either of us, or to the picture, it will be very, very bad for him."

"Hey, that's breaking the law," said Cole.

"And what are you racketeers doing, I'd like to know?" demanded Jessica.

Cole thought it was time to quit the pretense. He smiled as ingratiatingly as possible, and said, "Look here, I'm no thug. I'm a member of Justice, Inc.,"

"Never heard of it," said Jessica. But Marsden looked thoughtful.

"Justice, Inc.," explained Cole, "is a small band that tries to help people who are in trouble in such a way that the normal police help is cut off from them. The man at the head of it is Richard Benson, often called The Avenger."

"Never heard of him, either," said Jessica indifferently.

But now Marsden stopped looking thoughtful and looked enraged.

"That settles it," he ground out. "I've heard of Benson and of Justice, Inc. The Avenger heads a fine body of public-spirited citizens. When a hired killer like you tries to identify himself with a band like that, he deserves anything he gets. Take him to the wine cellar, Jess. He'll not get out of there in a hurry."

"Wait a minute!" said Cole. "I'm not kidding. I really am—"

"Shut up!" said the girl. "Turn around and go down the stairs again."

"Look—that gun'll go off if you don't stop—"

"I'll say it will go off. March!"

The wine cellar looked to Cole's eyes like something designed to hold another Prisoner of Zenda. It was a basement room, concrete-walled, with one tiny barred window and with a door that would have resisted the battering of a tank. The lock could have ornamented a bank vault.

It was maddeningly humiliating. Cole was going to have to call for help on his tiny belt radio. Trapped by a girl and a middle-aged man in a dressing gown! Mac and Smitty and Nellie would kid him for the rest of his life. Nevertheless, he'd have to yell for aid—

"Wonder if you have any more weapons on you," Jessica said, as he halted in the wine-cellar doorway.

With the gun trembling against his neck, Cole didn't dare do more than breathe gently. The girl's calm hand touched the hard small shield made by the radio.

"I don't know what this is," she said evenly, "but I'll take no chances."

"It's nothing to hurt anybody," said Cole, beginning to sweat. "It's perfectly harmless—"

"Maybe so. Take it off and pass it back to me."

"Now look here—"

The gun prodded harder. Cole felt the girl's whole hand

66

trembling from the strain of the moment. One tremble can twitch a trigger; and a man experienced with firearms is more terrified by an amateur's trembling fingers than the steady hand of a veteran.

He dragged out the little radio. It was taken from his grudging hand. Then the door was slammed solidly on him, and he was alone with a lot of wine bottles and some very bitter and helpless thoughts.

"Gee, she's a honey, though," he said after a minute. "She has almost as much nerve as she has good looks. Which is quite some."

Then he dismissed the thought of the girl and concentrated on trying to get out of his embarrassing predicament.

It was shortly to become a lot more than embarrassing.

At two o'clock in the afternoon Jessica Marsden brought Cole a tray of food, deftly balanced on her left hand, while she carried the gun in her right.

"It's about time you fed a guy," Cole grumbled. Then he grinned. He had a nice grin and knew it. He was handsome and knew that, too.

Neither did him any good.

"You're lucky to get any food at all," the girl said coldly. "I'm the cook, right now, and I don't like to work for cutthroats."

She started out, backing, her gun making a leap impossible on Cole's part.

"Wait a minute, Miss Marsden. What's your hurry? It's lonesome down here."

"That's too bad." Jessica started to shut the door.

"How long are you going to keep me here?"

"As long as your rotten crew molests my father," she said stonily. "Months, if necessary. Though I hope not. We don't like you."

"I'll get prison fever down here," Cole complained. "These cold, damp concrete walls—"

She didn't follow his gesture to the walls with her eyes. If she had, he would have risked a jump for the gun. The walls, incidentally, were quite dry and warm.

"Phone Richard Benson," pleaded Cole. "That isn't much to ask, is it? About two minutes could check my story that I work for The Avenger."

Jess Marsden was silent a moment. Then she reluctantly admitted, "We did phone Mr. Benson. There was no answer."

"Try him again and— What are you looking at?"

Her eyes snapped back to him. She'd been looking over his shoulder—which was still too much in his direction for him to try a break—and her face had lost some color.

Cole turned to look, too. The tiny barred window was behind him. He looked through the thick glass panes and saw what she had seen.

The legs of men on the lawn outside!

There were a lot of legs. Cole sorted them into eleven pairs. One pair was so thick they looked like twin tree trunks. A very heavy man owned those.

Jessica gasped and started to slam the door.

"So your friends have come," she said angrily.

"They're not my friends. Believe me!" Cole was beside himself with impatience at the thought of being cooped up here when trouble threatened.

"There are nearly a dozen men out there," he snapped. "Don't be a little dope, you little dope. Let me out of here. I'll help you."

"Sure! You'll help us—by pulling dirty work from the inside while they attack from the outside."

The door clicked shut. He sprang to it; put his ear to it. He could barely hear her quick footsteps as she ran up the basement stairs, though the steps must have been quite loud. That door was thick.

Cole jumped back to the window. It was too small to get through, even if there had been no bars. But, at least, he could hear through it. He smashed the glass out and listened.

He heard more glass breaking, down the house wall and overhead. The gang was breaking openly into the place this time. Tricks had failed. Now, they were smashing into the house!

Cole heard a shot over his head, muffled, then another. That would be the girl's gun. And he was all too sure that it wouldn't be heard outside that thick-walled house, even with a window broken open, so that help would come. He himself heard the shots through the floor, not through the window.

The shots were followed by a scream; and Cole, swearing impotently, flung himself against the door to get out. Of all the rotten breaks! To be shut in here while disaster occurred overhead.

He heard no more sound from above, now. Minutes passed. He kept on jamming against the door; there was nothing else to do. He had just banged against it for the dozenth time when it opened suddenly and he sprawled through the doorway onto the basement floor.

As he sprawled on the cement, he saw the legs of the man who had noiselessly and abruptly opened the door. They were incredibly thick legs, like tree trunks. He looked up. Then his spine seemed to freeze.

The legs belonged to the enormously fat man with the blue-black jowls who had shot the blond fellow at the crossroads. The man who had murdered his friend with the apologetic words: "Sorry, friend."

The fat man had a gun aimed at Cole's head and his forefinger was pressed hard against the trigger. He had been about to drill Cole. But then he recognized him.

"Well, shoot him," snarled a man next to the fat one. There were half a dozen in the basement. "If you don't, I will."

His gun, a foreign-looking automatic, swung into line.

"Wait!" said the fat man.

"What for? We can't stay here all day."

"This man—he was the one who trailed Harris that night. He's the one who got away with Harris' body and made me kill Harris so he couldn't talk."

His fat lips jerked with rage, then were calm again. Menacingly calm.

"What are you doing here?" he demanded.

Cole said nothing.

"He was helping the girl and her father, of course," said the man who held the foreign-looking gun. "That's the way his crowd operates. They help people. Even if they risk their stupid necks to do it—"

"He was locked in there," the fat man pointed out. "And he wouldn't have been locked up if he'd been considered as a friend."

"So?"

"So we'll take him along—"

Two more men piled downstairs. Cole stayed where he was, on hands and knees, not attempting to move or get up. His life hung by a very thin thread and he knew it.

"No trace of the picture," said one of the two, with an oath more feeling than interesting.

The fat man swore steadily for half a minute. "You're sure?"

"Of course, I'm sure. We took the place apart. The picture isn't in this house."

"Now I know we'll take this dog along," snarled the fat man, prodding Cole with his toe.

It was almost his last prod. Cole got the ankle behind the toe with a move so fast it almost defied the eye. Equally swiftly, he pulled. The fat man crashed down, and Cole got behind his bulk.

It was a fruitless move, because he had no gun, thanks to Jessica; and all the others were armed. Two covered

70

him, while a third bound him with phone wire ripped from the basement ceiling.

They carried him out to the driveway and piled him into a car there.

He saw Marsden and his daughter in another car. Both were unconscious. There was a red welt on the girl's forehead.

The two cars started, swung out to the road and headed for the thinly inhabited tip of Long Island lying to the east.

CHAPTER VIII

Watery Coffin!

The Avenger figured that he and Mac would be able to work undisturbed at Durban Vaughan's penthouse apartment. The police were still busy checking the actual murder site.

Dick and Mac went up an elevator to the top floor, then took the stairway to the penthouse. Dick rang the bell there, and there was no answer. It was odd that a place as big as he knew the penthouse to be would have no servant in it to answer the bell.

What he did not know at the time, and was to learn later, was that Vaughan, like Marsden, had had so much trouble with people trying to bribe his servants to get in that he had dismissed them all. Dick did know, however, that no one was opening the door, so he opened it himself.

Benson was probably the world's foremost authority on locks. And in his constant study of them, he had recently invented a master-key arrangement that would have given lockmakers nightmares if they'd known of it.

He carried with him a dozen key blanks, of the common, standard forms and sizes, which were stamped out of plastic. The plastic was of about the consistency of semi-hard rubber but did not have the elasticity of rubber. When a dent was made in the stuff, the dent stayed.

Benson had only to thrust the proper blank into a given lock, turn a little and draw the blank out. Then he cut notches where the dents showed, marked by the tumblers that did not give under pressure. He put the quickly made key back into the lock, turned gently and opened it.

They got into the murdered man's penthouse in about two minutes, this way; and after he had closed the door, Benson cut the notches off the plastic shank so that no one else could ever use it as a key.

Then they looked around for the "Diabolo."

"Diabolo" is a painting of a man and a woman dreamily approaching each other in late afternoon sun while the shadows of trees in the background form vaguely into the head of an approving devil.

And it didn't seem to be in Vaughan's penthouse.

"It wouldn't be under floor boards or in hollow places in the wall," commented Mac. " 'Tis a much bigger paintin' than 'The Dock,' which was rolled and stuck under a floor board at that vacant building. In fact, Muster Benson, I don't see how so big a picture could be hidden at all."

"It will be hidden in plain sight," said The Avenger.

They went over the living room. It was huge, elaborate, hung with many pictures. And Benson examined these paintings even though each depicted nothing like "Diabolo." He pulled each from the wall and looked behind it, and he sniffed at the face of each. It is possible to paint over a picture with soluble colors so that it looks like another picture entirely. Then the covering can be carefully washed off, revealing the original, unharmed, again.

But none of these pictures had the smell of fresh oils.

They split, then, and Mac took four rooms while Benson took four on the opposite side of the central corridor.

A microscopic search failed to reveal the painting.

There were four baths in the big apartment. They met at the end of the corridor, in the master's bath, where a glance was enough to show that no picture could be concealed there.

Dutifully, however, Mac's bleak blue eyes examined tile walls and floor. Then he opened the shower case, which was a very elaborate thing of plate glass and chromium, from floor to ceiling. It even had rubber stripping around the door, like the door of a refrigerator, so that no water got out while a bather sprayed himself. It looked like an upended coffin with a nozzle at the top.

"Vaughan did himself well, I'm thinkin'," said the Scot disapprovingly. Mac spent a nickel like he parted with a toe; and this glistening shower cabinet had cost an awful lot of nickels. "Why a mon can't take a shower with only shower currrtains around him is more than I know."

Dick went out to the corridor, pale eyes narrowed in thought.

"Well, the 'Diabolo' is not here. That is certain. So it is either up in Vaughan's Connecticut home or hidden where no one can ever find it."

"Whoosh!" said Mac. "I'd admire to see the skurlie that could hide anything where you couldn't find—"

He stopped. Benson's hand was on his forearm, and Mac shut his teeth hard on the yelp at what The Avenger must have thought was no finger pressure at all.

Benson nodded down the corridor toward the door. Someone was trying a key in it.

"Visitors, huh?" whispered Mac. "Do ye think it may be the gang that—"

He didn't finish it. There were voices outside, careless

75

and rather loud, not the voices of anyone trying to sneak in. Also, the key had turned the lock bolt smoothly, leading Dick and Mac to believe that it must be the regular key to this place.

"Police," nodded Mac. "It's all right, chief."

The Avenger said nothing. His eyes were like pale holes in his calm face as he stared at the entering men.

Two were in police uniform, two were in plain clothes, and there was a sleek-looking, jauntily authoritative fellow at their head who appeared to have come from the district attorney's office.

"What the—" exclaimed the sleek-looking man, staring at the two in the corridor. He had very dark hair and eyes, was quite the playboy type at first glance; yet he handled himself with the air of a man who always knows just what he is doing.

"Oh!" he said suddenly. His dark eyes went friendly. "You must be Richard Benson. There's only one man with eyes that light under hair that black, who might be found in a dead man's rooms. Did you turn up any clues, Mr. Benson?"

The Avenger's face was like that of a sphinx as he watched the five come down the hall toward him. His eyes were unreadable.

"No clues," he said quietly. "I don't seem to place you, Mr.—"

"The name is Add—Addfield. I'm in the D.A.'s office. New there. But I've heard about you, sir."

"So have we," said one of the plain-clothes men. "It's a pleasure to have you work with us, sir."

"You have come here as a matter of routine," said The Avenger. "But have you anything in particular in mind to look for in your regular searching?"

The sleek, dark chap nodded pleasantly.

"Vaughan's private records, as I suppose you know, sir, disclose that he recently bought Dubois' 'Diabolo.'

We'd like a look at it, among other things. If you'd show us where you had searched, it might save duplication of effort."

He was moving easily toward the two, with his men behind him, when The Avenger's voice stopped them.

Benson's voice didn't seem to change a note, but suddenly it was as deadly as the thrust of a bushmaster.

"Stay where you are!"

The five stopped. In The Avenger's hands had appeared the two seemingly toy weapons which were all he ever armed himself with. In his right hand was a slim little throwing knife with a hollow tube for a handle. He called it, with glacial affection, Ike. In the left hand, he held an equally slim, streamlined revolver that had a special silencer and a .22 slug. This, he had named Mike.

These were all Dick held against five men. But Mac-Murdie knew that they were plenty! And the five must have heard something of Mike and Ike, too, because none moved and none tried for his own weapon.

"But Muster Benson," began Mac, bewildered at the shift.

"These are the men we're after, Mac," said Benson evenly. "Look at that 'patrolman's' shoes. Black, but decidedly not regulation. Look at the cut of the other's coat."

"All right," snarled the sleek dark man suddenly and loudly. "You win. We're not cops. So what are you planning to do about it? You and that hatpin and pea shooter—"

It was well done and well timed. The snarling, loud voice hid all sound of the stealthy footsteps behind Mac and Benson!

Just at the last instant, The Avenger's quick brain sensed something wrong, and his sharp ears caught a ghost of a sound in spite of the dark fellow's clever camouflage of noise.

But it wasn't soon enough. Benson whirled like light,

staggered as a gun barrel slapped down on his head, then fell as a second terrific blow descended!

Mac whirled, too, ducking at the same time as a veteran rough-and-tumble fighter should. He got a glimpse of three men grinning at him without humor, then was slugged by the dark, sleek chap to whom he'd been forced to present his back.

He went down, too.

For once, The Avenger, being human after all and not quite a perfect machine, had overlooked something. That was the French windows in the penthouse which led to a terrace. A careful leader could send three men along a ledge to that terrace to enter at the rear, while he and four followers came openly in the front door. He could thus completely surprise even a smart enemy, perhaps to be encountered in the penthouse.

The sleek dark man had been smart; and Justice, Inc., had been surprised.

Mac's first conscious sensation as he struggled back from oblivion was freezing cold from the knees down. And steadily and rather swiftly, the chill was creeping upward.

He blinked and opened his eyes. It took a few seconds to focus them; but when he really did begin to see, he tried at once to yell and he tried to struggle.

He couldn't do either.

He was gagged so that he could scarcely breathe, let alone yell. Also he was bound at ankles, waist and wrists. But his bonds seemed to give a little, queerly, when he tried to break free.

The reason for that was soon apparent. Another figure was lashed to his the same way—arms, waist and ankles.

"Muster Benson," the Scot tried to say. The result, through the gag, was kind of a croak.

The Avenger's eyelids were opening.

Benson was one of those men who woke from sleep

instantly, clearly, in possession of all his powers. Unconsciousness is an artificial sleep. He snapped out of this in almost the same way, and his pale eyes took in the situation.

It was some situation!

The two men were bound rigidly together, wedged upright, in the glass-and-chromium shower cabinet in the master bathroom. They were standing in a rising flood. Over their heads, water poured. The shower had been turned on full force—the cold water, mercifully. If the hot had been used, they'd have died slowly and dreadfully.

They could thank the dark chap for at least this favor, though it was certainly little of a favor because they were going to die slowly and dreadfully anyway.

The water was up to their waists, now. Some trickled out around the tight-fitting door, but not enough to relieve the flood within the cabinet.

Mac fought his bonds again, but stopped at a pressure from The Avenger. Benson's eyes, showing no emotion even in this crisis, went to the spouting nozzle, overhead. The stream would easily fill the plate-glass cabinet from floor to the air vent at the top of the door, far above their heads, in four or five minutes.

The water was up to their chests, now!

Mac glared at the place where the handles should have been. The hot water knob was there all right. The cold water knob was gone, leaving only a little metal nub, so that the flood couldn't have been turned off with anything less than a pipe wrench.

Mac gave himself up for lost.

"Downed in my bath," he thought with grisly humor. "Weel, I've always said too many baths were weakenin'."

The water was up to his chin, which meant that The Avenger would be keeping his nostrils above it only by standing on tiptoe, for Mac was inches taller than Dick.

Mac could feel Benson doing something or other with his feet.

"Ye'll make a soggy angel, Fergus MacMurdie," he told himself. It was one of the dour Scot's crazy traits that when things were at their worst a mad streak of optimism cropped up in his otherwise pessimistic philosophy. "That is—if ye're slated for heaven. Because the chief's wigglin' his feet mighty funny, and I canna' believe he'd take to wings and a harp in any confounded shower cabinet."

The water went over his chin, which means that the chief by now would be holding his breath with his face submerged.

Then Mac caught the meaning of Benson's foot moving.

"The drain!"

And even as he thought it, he felt current around his ankles, and the water level began to recede rapidly, though the flood continued to pour from the overhead nozzle.

There was a porcelain hand grip waist high in the wall of the cabinet. The Avenger tapped with fingertips to MacMurdie's palm, "Kneel down with me."

They couldn't exactly kneel. The space of the cabinet was too cramped. But they could sag straight down with hinged legs, now that the water was almost out of the cabinet that had so nearly proved to be their coffin. Benson got his face to the hand grip and managed to slide his gag off.

"They stuffed a towel down the drain to stop it up," Dick said, voice as emotionless as if he were talking about an electric-light bill. "However, they didn't think to screw the metal grill back in place. I got a shoe off and managed to fish the towel out with my toes."

Mac croaked into his gag. What he wanted to say, and couldn't, was: "Sure. Just like that. As if just anybody who tried it could reach down two or three inches and clamp onto a bit of cloth hard enough to draw it up, after the way that gang must have jammed it down to make it a water-tight plug! And all with just the strength in his toes!"

There might be another man living whose steel muscles were so trained, even to the sinew of his feet, that he could perform a miracle like that. But Mac would have to see this other man to believe it.

The Avenger's arms and hands were working, now, and the Scot knew they'd soon be free.

Benson's hands were of the slim, rarely supple type that could be so held as to be but a fraction of an inch larger than the wrists above. Therefore, he could work out of almost any rope bonds if given time—which he was now given because death by drowning no longer threatened.

Mac felt Benson's arms suddenly move free, and after that he himself was untied. The Avenger broke the plate-glass cabinet door because that handle, too, had been taken off by the methodical killers, so it couldn't be opened from inside.

"The murderin' skurlies!" were Mac's words. "The cold-blooded torturers! The murrr—"

"Good way to kill us noiselessly and meanwhile have plenty of time to escape," Dick said, almost approvingly.

His tone was as calm as ever. Would anything ever break this man's iron repression? Mac wondered. But it left a man ice-cold to reason clearly in an emergency.

Benson started toward the door to the outer stairs, and he started fast.

"Connecticut," he said over his shoulder. But that was enough for Mac.

The "Diabolo" had not been in Vaughan's office vault. It had not been here. There was one other likely place for it, and that was Vaughan's Connecticut home.

The sleek, dark man and his gang would have the sense to figure that out in a hurry and must, even now, be on their way up there. And in the Connecticut place this crew—eight of them—would find Smitty and Nellie, unwarned, ripe for the trap!

CHAPTER IX

Crooks vs. Crooks

It was a very nice afternoon for a drive to the country. Nellie and Smitty were not expecting any trouble. So they made a jaunt of it, though they let no grass grow under the wheels.

Vaughan's country place looked peaceful and inviting in the warm afternoon sun. There was a big L-shaped house. There was a garage and also a small barn, for the place had been a working farm.

Smitty pressed the front doorbell with a ponderous finger. They both heard the bell ring inside, but there was no answer to the summons.

"There must be somebody here," said Nellie.

"Well, if there is, he's in a coma," retorted Smitty, jabbing the bell again. "Maybe Vaughan came out so seldom that he saved expenses by not keeping servants here."

"Goof," said Nellie.

"What do you mean, goof? If a guy only comes to a

place one or two days a month, he might shut it up between times and bring a servant or two with him."

"Look at the lawn," Nellie said. "Nicely cut. Look at the flower-beds. Well-tended. It's a full-time job for at least one man to take care of all this. There must be a caretaker around."

"Well, he's not here now." Smitty tried the door.

It was unlocked.

The giant and the half-pint blonde entered the house warily. Unlocked doors, they had long ago discovered, were something to be careful about.

The first thing they saw was the blood on the floor.

The door opened into a large hall that was furnished more as an auxiliary sitting room than an entrance hall. There were a few rugs, but mainly the polished floor was bare. And right next to the door, the dark surface was messed up with a small sticky puddle, not yet coagulated.

They looked at each other. Then they looked around some more.

The place had been turned upside down.

Pictures were askew on the walls; and, of course, there were many pictures, since that had been the owner's business. Cushions were off divan and padded chairs. Drapes were half yanked down over the end window.

They stepped to a side door and looked into a large living room. This was in the same state of upheaval.

"So," said Nellie, "there is a caretaker. Or was one."

Smitty nodded soberly. The wrecked place, and the pool of blood, told a plain story.

Some gang had come here, pressed the bell, slugged the caretaker when he opened the door, and then searched the house with a destructive thoroughness.

There could have been only one thing for which such a search would be made. That was the picture "Diabolo."

"We're too late," mourned the giant. "They must have gotten the thing, if it was here to get. No painting that big could stay hidden after such a combing."

"I wonder," Nellie said.

She was looking at the wall near the front door. Looking at a large picture there, the first your eyes rested on when you stepped inside the house.

"Now who's the goof?" demanded Smitty. "As if a painting as big as 'Diabolo' could stay hidden after—"

He stopped. Nellie had stepped to the picture and was looking at it more thoughtfully than ever. It was a landscape, just fairly well done; nothing to draw a second glance. There was a good, but not expensive, frame around it.

"That's queer," said the tiny blonde.

"What's queer about it?" said Smitty.

"What do you think of that as a work of art?"

"It's nothing to write home about," Smitty began. Then he started to get the idea, too.

"Here's a man whose business is buying and selling pictures," mused Nellie. "Presumably, he is a connoisseur. He would want only the best for his own home. Yet, he hangs this half-baked thing, of a kind you could get by the dozen, in a prominent place in his hall."

Her small hand went out, and she flipped the picture around on its hook so that it presented its back to their gaze and its front to the wall.

Smitty sighed. For a moment he'd entertain the imaginative notion that Vaughan had hidden the "Diabolo" by having another picture painted on the back of the famous canvas and hanging it so that the new picture seemed the regular one. But the back of this mediocre landscape wasn't "Diabolo." It was just blank canvas.

Nellie, however, wasn't sighing. She touched that blank fabric.

"Looks awfully clean for an old canvas," she said.

And then Smitty breathed again. His first idea had hit the mark. The back of the canvas was not canvas. It was cheesecloth. And when this was ripped away, the object of their trip up here was revealed.

The "Diabolo."

"By gosh," said Smitty. "You do have a fairly lucid moment, now and then—"

Both turned to listen. And the sound that had stopped Smitty came again.

A faint, desperate cry from the direction of the barn.

Nellie dropped the picture. Smitty ran out the door and toward the barn, with the little blonde on his heels.

"Get back in the house, will you?" Smitty rasped. "There might be trouble out here."

"So what?" Nellie panted. "If there is, you'll probably need a nurse to—"

They plunged into the barn. After the sun, the interior of the building was gloomy. It took a moment to see the man who had cried out frantically for help. Then they saw him, at the far side of the barn.

He was a stocky fellow in overalls, with dried blood on the side of his head. He lay on the dirt floor, with hands and legs tightly roped so that he couldn't move.

Here was the caretaker.

Smitty reached the man in two jumps. He opened his knife as he bent down.

The man whispered. "Watch out! They're—"

Nellie yelped a warning.

From the shadows came an avalanche of men! The avalanche went over Smitty like a landslide over a big tree; and he went down.

He heard Nellie call his name, then heard some man yell in a way that meant the little blonde had executed one of her efficient jujitsu tricks.

Usually when a man is down, with such odds against him, he is also out. But not Smitty. The big fellow fought almost as well from a prone position as he did on his feet.

Feet were searching for his head, earnestly trying to kick his brains out. He grabbed a couple of the feet and squeezed. The owners yelled as something like a vise made jelly of their toes, and they hopped off to sit down and moan.

Legs swarmed around as more men gathered to club at the prone giant. Smitty gathered as many legs in his vast arms as he could—and sat up. As he sat up, about four men sat down. Then he could rise.

He bellowed as he saw two men battering at Nellie. The diminutive blonde had ducked everything so far; then one of the two tagged her satiny cheek while she was engaged in tangling the other in his own feet.

Smitty tore loose from the rest and got to the man who had hit Nellie. The big fellow smacked this one so forcefully that he described an arc through a dozen feet of space and smashed against the barn wall so hard that a board came loose and fell outside.

Then the crew started shooting.

"Back of me!" roared Smitty.

Nellie got behind him. Smitty plunged forward, caught two men who were ahead of their fellows and held them in front of him, each encircled by a huge arm.

It wasn't going to do the trick. It began to look as if they wouldn't leave that barn alive!

This bunch of thugs had seen them enter the house. They had deliberately made the bound and helpless caretaker yell for help so Smitty and Nellie would come to his rescue; then they ambushed them.

Smitty felt a couple of giant punches in his left side. Two of the gang had worked around so they could shoot past their two kicking fellows and get at Smitty's vast torso. The bulletproof celluglass had saved him. He heard Nellie say, "Oof!" and saw her almost fall as a slug hammered her sheathed body.

Five men were between Smitty and Nellie and the door to which they'd been backing. The giant glared at them and saw, over their shoulder, another man running toward the barn.

Smitty flung the two men he'd been holding, at the

87

five, and dug into his pockets. He got a handful of little gas pellets and threw them.

But as he threw, he heard the running man outside yell: "Lam! It's the law!"

The five stopped shooting at the big fellow and the blonde, and they duly "lammed." They may not even have known any trouble in the form of anaesthetic pellets had been thrown in their vicinity; anyhow, they raced into the open before the fumes rose. So they were all right, and Nellie and Smitty got the dosage themselves.

This was all right, too. Each had a small noseclip to keep out such fumes, with a measured oxygen supply that would let them breathe till the fumes dissipated. But while they were putting these things on, something else unforeseen happened.

A blue-uniformed officer appeared in the barn doorway.

"Well, we're sure glad to see you—" Smitty began. Then he stopped with a strangling cough. He shouldn't have opened his mouth to talk in the midst of MacMurdie's knock-out gas. But he would have stopped anyway, in surprise at what the officer did.

The rescuing cop made no response to Smitty's welcome. As a greeting, he slid the barn door tightly shut, and the giant heard the creak of a hasp as the door was padlocked.

"Hey!" Smitty felt like yelling indignantly—but didn't.

He went to the door and shook it violently. Two bullets ripped splinters from the door a foot from him.

He glared at Nellie. "The fools think we're gunmen and are centering their attention on keeping us trapped in here while the real crooks get away!" his eyes said. But the small blonde's eyes had a different expression.

Smitty went to the rear of the barn where his tremendous blow had knocked off a board with a man's body. The instant he showed his big head at the tall, slender opening where the board had been, another burst of slugs sent him ducking back out of sight.

The gas had risen upward toward the lofty barn roof so that it was possible to take off the clips.

"Those idiots!" raved Smitty. "I never saw cops so dumb!"

"They're not cops," Nellie said. "That uniform—it's the uniform of the New York police, not anything you'd see in rural Connecticut. They're phonies."

Smitty took a minute to digest that. So they were crooks. And the first set were crooks. Why had one set chased the other? Rival gangs, apparently, but—

Nellie had an eye to a knothole in the side of the barn toward the house.

"They're going in the house," she said. "We left the 'Diabolo' lying right on the hall floor where they can't help but see it. That's what they're after, of course. Well, it's gone now!"

Smitty began sniffing. There was still an acrid sting of the anaesthetic gas in the air. But this new odor went over that. A smell of fire!

At the same time the crackle of flames came to their ears, and gray smoke drifted in front of the knothole through which Nellie was staring.

For a moment, though, Nellie almost ignored the smoke. She had caught a glimpse of a dark, sleek man, one of the gang of pseudo-police, through the open doorway of the house. And she was remembering where she had seen that sinister playboy before.

Then Smitty was clutching at her arm.

"They've fired the barn!" he snapped. "We've got to get out of here!"

He picked up a four-foot length of log from the wood stacked for Vaughan's fireplaces. He rammed the door, and again was answered by slugs ripping perilously close around him. He tried the siding at both ends and the back. Bullets!

"Get ready to dodge lead," he called grimly to Nellie. Then he went on battering at the siding of one end, regardless of the bullets menacing him from outside. He was hit in the body half a dozen times. Splinters stung his head, where the real danger lay! There was no bulletproof celluglass over his skull.

Four boards came off under his pounding. The opening revealed three men crouched in tall grass and pouring lead at him.

"O.K.!" gasped Smitty through the gathering smoke. "Shooting or no shooting, we're getting out—" His voice tailed off into silence, as he saw one of the three guards.

He was a man who must have weighed nearly three hundred pounds, with a blue-jowled face that Smitty knew he had seen before.

In the Pink Room of the Coyle Hotel.

The sound of shooting was drowned suddenly in a burst of sirens from three cars. Nellie sped back to her knothole.

"They're leaving!" she cried. "They're jumping into their cars as if the army was after them!"

She didn't have to say it. Smitty had seen the three waddle toward the driveway at the warning sound of the horns. At least, the fat man had waddled, at an incredibly fast clip. The other two shoved to get ahead of him.

"Oh!" said Nellie suddenly in complete comprehension.

One car had appeared in the entrance of the driveway. From the leading edge of each front fender of this car came little rosy bursts of flame as twin machine guns, aimed wheel-high, swept a leaden hail at the tires of the three cars.

The tires stayed up. They were the military type, self-sealing, that could take indefinite piercing without harm. The three cars jounced over open fields for the road. And the one big limousine hesitated like a live thing, debating whether to go on after its quarry or stay to help Smitty and Nellie.

Nellie thought she could see rare uncertainty in the pale eyes of The Avenger at the wheel of the car. She screamed: "Don't bother about us! We can get out! Nail those guys!"

It couldn't be heard over the roar of the flames and through the thick windows of the car. So the limousine kept on to the barn. One rule was paramount in Ben's career: The lives of his aides came first.

The car crashed through the sliding door as if it had been paper. Mac, eyes blazing, flung open the rear door.

"In!" he barked.

Nellie hopped in. But Smitty ran to where the bound caretaker still lay, with the unconscious member of the first gang—the one Smitty had smashed against the side of the barn—beside him. The big fellow hoisted them both into the rear of the car with Nellie and himself.

The car shot backward through the leaping flames to safety.

But the gang with the fat man and the sleek dark man had escaped.

"The picture?" said Benson calmly, face as calm as though nothing adventurous had occurred. " 'Diabolo'?"

"Gone by now," sighed Smitty. "We left it so they could not miss finding it. So—"

"I'm not sure it's gone," Nellie interrupted. "I didn't see it carried out by any of that bunch when they ran in answer to the siren warning."

"Of course, they'd take it," said Smitty. "That's what they came for. Why wouldn't they take it, with nothing to stop them?"

"It won't hurt to look," Nellie pointed out.

So she stepped into the hall.

The picture was there, on the hall floor.

"What in the blazes—" gaped Smitty.

The gang that had trapped them in the barn had raised Heaven and earth to get to this picture. Having gotten to it, they seemed suddenly to have decided they didn't want it, after all. It was mad. Insane!

The Avenger took it with him. He took the unconscious member of the first gang in to Bleek Street, too, after tending the caretaker who had been slugged and bound.

The affair of the looted masterpieces was being beautifully consistent in one regard at least. It was continuing to yield absolutely no results to the most diligent investigating.

CHAPTER X

Dates of Destruction!

Back at headquarters, they tried to make something of a bunch of puzzling, apparently nonsensical crime pieces.

Just after they'd returned from Connecticut, Cole Wilson had called from Long Island that he was on his way back. So they could dismiss worry over his inexplicable and lengthy absence and devote their time to the puzzle.

The Avenger, in telling of what had happened to him and Mac at Vaughan's penthouse, had described the sleek, dark leader.

Nellie nodded vigorously.

"I saw him, too. And I've seen him before. Not for long, but long enough so I ought to remember."

"He gave his name as Addfield," said Benson. "Probably an alias."

That was enough for the half-pint blonde.

"I've got it! Smitty, you remember the dark fellow with the woman in white in the foyer of the Pink Room?"

"Yeah," said Smitty.

"This must be that man! He gave his name then as Addington. Richard Addington. He and that woman were the only two who noticed when Teebo disappeared from in front of an open window."

"Only the woman noticed it," replied Smitty. "Addington claimed not to have seen anything."

"Anyhow—that's him. He's in this up to his neck. Maybe he could tell how Teebo died."

"If Teebo did die," Smitty said slowly.

"Again?" sighed Nellie.

"Listen. Back at that barn I saw a fat guy. And if it wasn't Teebo, I'm a gorilla."

"That's an unfortunate remark," said Nellie, eyes going over Smitty's mountainous bulk.

"Why, you little ingrate!" gasped Smitty. "After I saved your life back at that barn—"

"Go on. You'd be there yet if it hadn't been for the boss. Save my life, indeed!"

The quiet but dominant voice of The Avenger recalled them to the task at hand.

"You say this Addington was in the foyer near Teebo at the time of Teebo's disappearance?"

"Yes," said Nellie.

"Could Addington have pushed the fat man out of that window?"

"I don't see how," said Nellie. "They were twenty feet apart."

Mac approached them. The Scotchman had been examining the "Diabolo" with X-rays and other testing devices as the fake picture, "The Dock," had been tested. But Mac looked perplexed instead of satisfied.

"This painting," he said, "is no fake."

"What?" said Smitty.

The others stared. They'd all taken it for granted that it would be a phony, just as the supposed Gauguin was a phony.

"It's the real thing," said Mac. "It has been touched

94

up in just one spot—this lavender shadow in the background—but that's all. It's a genuine Dubois."

"Then why didn't that crowd that trapped Nellie and me in the barn take the picture with them?" demanded Smitty.

"It's as if all they wanted was a look at it," said Nellie. "But that doesn't make sense."

"Maybe it does." The Avenger said quietly. They looked at him, but he didn't trouble to explain. He summed up:

"There are definitely two separate gangs mixed up in this business. They are enemies—not connected with one another.

"A fat man named Teebo apparently fell to his death, and yet is seen shortly after with the rival gang.

"This second gang appears to trail the first, trying to get back the pictures that the first sells. Yet, in the case of 'Diabolo,' at least, having got to the picture, the second gang doesn't take it after all.

The leader of the second gang, Addington, or Addfield, was present at the supposed death of Teebo.

"Sometimes the paintings dealt in by the first gang are fakes; sometimes they are genuine. It doesn't seem to matter to the second crowd. They go after the fakes as desperately as they go after the originals.

"One of the second gang, killed by his own man, carried a queer ruler calibrated in uneven spaces, with a single mark on the back of it.

"In one picture we've seen, 'The Dock,' the color of the fisher lad's nose was different from the original. In this other, 'Diabolo,' a spot of color in the background has been deepened. Both variations are color variations."

They waited for The Avenger to go on; but he didn't go on. He tossed these fragments of facts forth, and then stopped, his pale eyes like colorless holes in his expressionless face as he arranged the pieces in his quick brain.

Perhaps the arrangement meant something to him; it didn't to Mac or Nellie or Smitty.

Then they forgot deductions for a moment because Cole Wilson returned. And in tow he had a girl so pretty that Smitty's eyes made Nellie kick him covertly in the shins.

Cole introduced her as Miss Jessica Marsden. Then, coloring sheepishly while the girl looked apologetic, he told of his embarrassing capture at the Marsden home, followed by the attack of the gang under the leadership of the fat man.

"They took Miss Marsden and her father away in one car, and me in another," said Cole. "The car I was in dropped quite a distance behind the first; I guess they didn't want it to be apparent that they were trailing each other. I pressed my arm hard against my side and smashed one of Mac's handy little anaesthetic pellets, got clear of the telephone wire they'd tied me up with, and that was that. I dove out just as they were coming around again, and I started walking to the nearest town where I could rent a car. In a couple of miles I overtook Miss Marsden."

The Avenger's pale eyes swung to the girl's face.

"The men who'd taken Dad and me, deliberately set me loose," explained Jessica Marsden. "They shoved me out of the car and told me they'd get in touch with me later."

"That means they intend to hold your father in exchange for something they want," Benson said. "It is a picture?"

"Yes. 'The Princess,' by Vernier."

"Then they'll make you give up the picture in exchange for your father's life."

"I know," said Jessica, looking desperate. "And I don't know where the picture is."

"You don't?"

"No. I haven't any idea where it is. All I know is that Dad hid it somewhere. So I won't be able to save him by giving up the picture. That's why I came here. For help."

96

She looked at Wilson. "I'm so sorry I mistook you for one of the gang and didn't let you try to help us. I was stupid."

"Just a minute," said Smitty, looking bewildered. "You say this fat boy led the gang that attacked the Marsden house. We saw him about that time up in Connecticut."

"You saw him just afterward," said Cole. "He had on radio earphones when I busted Mac's sleeping pill. I heard him say, 'We're to go to the Connecticut place on the double and join the others.' Then I let them have it."

"They joined the others, all right," said Nellie grimly. The fiery trap that had almost closed over them was still in her mind.

Then she remembered something.

"Say! The fellow Smitty knocked out—the one we lugged here from the barn. Why don't we see what he has to say for himself?"

The Avenger nodded. "Yes. Get him, Smitty. He's on the second floor."

There were beautifully furnished living quarters on the second floor. Also, there was a room with barred windows and a special door guaranteed to hold anyone a prisoner. Smitty went to this room and came back to the top-floor headquarters with their captive.

They all looked at him with a feeling of disappointment.

The man was an ordinary crook, defiant, not too intelligent-looking, tough.

"What a yegg!" murmured Nellie.

"Yeah?" snarled the man. "Well, lemme tell you, lady—"

Smitty had one vast hand on the nape of the man's neck. He squeezed just a little, and the man squawked and became silent.

The Avenger hypnotized the fellow.

Few pairs of eyes had such effect as the pale, glacial

orbs of Richard Benson. It was a rare person who did not succumb to The Avenger's will after a few minutes of staring reluctantly into their cold, clear depths and listening to a quiet flow of words spoken in a soft monotone by the even, dominant voice.

This man did not have a strong will. He went under in record time.

"What is your name?" said Benson, when the man was completely in a trance.

"Charles Minz," said the man in a dull, mechanical tone.

"For whom are you working?"

"A couple guys by the name of Teebo and Zara."

"Teebo is dead. Didn't you know that?"

"That's what we heard. But Zara came around, all burned up, and said Teebo wasn't dead but had just double-crossed us and left. So I dunno."

"You're in a fake-picture racket, aren't you?"

"Some are phonies, some are the real stuff."

"How do you get them?"

"Teebo and Zara have a pipeline out of France."

"You sold a painting to Durban Vaughan."

"Yeah. Teebo did."

"Then your gang killed Vaughan to try to get it back. Why was that?"

"We didn't knock him off. That was the other gang."

"What other gang?"

"We don't just know," said the man in his dull voice. "All we know is that we sell a picture; then this other gang tries to get their mitts on it. Highjackers, I guess."

"Maybe you didn't try to get Vaughan's picture back, at his gallery; but you certainly tried to get it at the Connecticut place."

"Yeah. By then, we had it doped out that this stuff we'd been handling must be worth a lot more than we knew; worth so much that these other mugs killed Vaughan to get his picture away from him. So we thought we'd

98

get it ourselves and see who offered how much for it. But before we'd found it, the other gang got there. We thought it was the cops, at first, and lammed. Later we caught on, but we'd have beat it anyway because they had us about three to one."

"Then you have no idea why they want these pictures?"

"Nope!"

"Who else have you sold pictures to besides Marsden and Vaughan?"

"A rich guy named Ellsworth, is the only other one I know. There've been a lot more, but I wasn't in on 'em."

The Avenger decided that this was all he could get from the fellow. His tone changed, and his eyes relaxed their almost physical grip on the man, as he said: "All right. Smitty, I think the police might be interested in our friend, Charles Minz. Turn him over to them."

The man's ratlike eyes blinked a couple of times; then he glared around him. He didn't know just what had happened, but he sensed that something had. Something that shouldn't have.

"Hey! What'd you do to me? You—"

Smitty dragged him out to wait in the private Justice, Inc., cooler, till the police could come for him.

"We got one slight bit of information, anyway," Benson said. "Winton Ellsworth, the Wall Street man, was also sold a painting. We can follow that lead."

But it developed that they'd have had this lead anyhow, because, just then, Josh and Rosabel came in with a report on their long and laborious news sifting. The glints in their eyes told that something tremendously significant had come out of the search.

"Well, we sure found something," said Josh. "Man, what we got!"

They listened to an account of happenings that were too pat to be just coincidental, and which had such grim undertones that all found themselves almost holding their breaths.

Josh unfolded a sheet of note paper. The Negro's hands showed whitish highlights because he clutched the paper so hard.

"Three art collectors have reported attempted burglaries in the past ten weeks," said Josh. "They are Alfred Swazey, Winton Ellsworth and James Gates. As far as I could tell from reading the accounts, no one of them voluntarily reported to the police. It was a servant who reported in each case. It was as if the master didn't want the police to know."

"Which makes it at least possible," Rosabel added, "that perhaps many more collectors have been attacked and have said nothing."

Josh nodded and went on.

"Swazey said the thieves undoubtedly were after an ermine coat his wife had just bought. Ellsworth thought they were after cash in his bedroom wall safe. Gates said they were probably trying to steal his wife's jewels. But in each case"—Josh paused and stared at The Avenger—"in each case the entry was through a window in whatever room or hall the owner kept his choice paintings."

"Of course," said Mac. "After the pictures. We knew that before."

Josh didn't even look at the Scot.

"And in each case," he said, "nothing was missing!"

The Avenger's eyes were like glacial ice.

"They broke in, stayed for no one knows how long and went out again without taking the pictures," said Josh.

"Wait a minute," Nellie protested. "Remember these paintings are stolen goods and the collectors know it. They couldn't report their loss to the police, even if they had been taken. So we don't know—"

"We do know," said Josh. "In each case, a servant reported the burglary. In each case, the servant would

100

surely have noticed if a picture—either a camouflaged masterpiece or one hanging openly—was gone from the wall. Such was never reported. So such never happened."

"They broke in and examined the paintings, but they did not take them," Dick mused. "It was about what I expected."

"Mon, ye might have expected it, but to the rest of us 'tis without meanin' whateverrr—"

"Go on, Josh, there is more, isn't there?" Dick said.

"I'll say there's more! Something tremendous. Something terrific!"

Josh's hand trembled a little so that the sheet of paper rattled.

"The gang broke into Winton Ellsworth's place July 8th. On July 10th, the King Dam and its powerhouse, in Tennessee, were blown up."

"Aluminum," said Smitty, eyes hard.

"Yes. A new aluminum plant had just been completed. It was just about to go into production when the explosion occurred. It will take months to rebuild the dam and the power plant. That's one coincidence. It might not mean anything by itself, but it isn't by itself.

"Swazey's house was entered on July 19th. On July 22nd, the Lorenville, Indiana, powder plant went up with a burst that smashed windows eight miles away. That was our second largest new powder plant."

They were all silent now. There wasn't any need to comment; this spoke for itself.

"Gates' place was burglarized—with nothing taken—on August 1st. On August 2nd four ships loaded with wheat sank at their Hoboken docks. The ships are already almost reconditioned, but the wheat is a thing of the past."

The Avenger's eyes were terrible in their icy colorlessness. The rest stared at him almost in awe and waited for him to decide what was to be done next.

101

The affair was clearing, now, with a vengeance! Somehow, the purloined masterpieces smuggled out of Europe contained messages, all right, though it was still impossible to guess the manner of it. They were messages of death and destruction.

"The Dock," here in this room, held such a hidden message. It was vital that the picture fall, for a little while, into the hands of the gang that lived on the heels of the picture racketeers. That was why the blond fellow, Harris, had taken such chances to get hold of it.

"The Princess," hidden by Marsden, contained such a message. So the gang had been driven to the desperate expedient of kidnaping a multimillionaire to get hold of the picture and get hold of it fast.

"Diabolo," also here in this room, spelled out foreign enemy instructions. And—here The Avenger's face grew more terrible still—the "Diabolo" had been deciphered!

The gang had had it in its possession at Vaughan's country home long enough to read it. Then they had left it. That was why they weren't interested in possession. They didn't care whether a picture was a fake or an original worth many thousands of dollars. A hundred thousand dollars was nothing compared to the stakes for which they played.

So they had carelessly left the "Diabolo" where it lay.

But first they had deciphered its message!

What would result from that? What catastrophe would grow out of it, and was there any way to stop it?

These thoughts were plain in the faces of the members of Justice, Inc., as they stared at their leader for a plan of action.

But it was Jessica Marsden who suggested it.

"This is all horrible," she said diffidently. "And, of course, it comes before any personal considerations. But I . . . I hope you're not forgetting that my father is in danger of his life. And I'm wondering if you can't progress as fast in this mystery by trying to trace him and 'The Princess' as you could in any other line of action."

The Avenger's eyes turned their pale gaze her way. Then he nodded.

"Yes. As well that way as any other. Cole, you and Mac go with Miss Marsden to her home. It will be there that the gang will try to contact her, to arrange for trading her father's life for the picture."

The three went out. Dick Benson picked up one of the battery of phones on his vast desk. This one, Smitty knew, was a direct line, always open, to Washington.

Dick called an unlisted number in the state department. The name he called, after a few seconds' wait, was one to command respect. Benson didn't bother with underlings.

"Richard Addington," he said. "Average height, a little more than average weight, very dark hair and eyes, sleek. He looks like a playboy and a rather weak one at that—except when he's on a job. Then his face hardens till you realize that he is smart, ruthless, a powerful enemy. Do you have anything on this man?"

The reply was given in about eighty seconds.

"A naturalized citizen," was the state department's answer. "Roland Ardmore, alias Richard Addington, alias a dozen more names. Suspected of being a foreign espionage agent, but not once has any definite proof of it been found. He is watched constantly. His mail is inspected, and he is followed. Now and then, however, he has managed to shake off his trailers. He is very clever."

"Associates?" said Benson.

"There is only one known, and that one has not been thoroughly checked. All we know is that his name is Teebo."

The Avenger stared at the phone, his face and eyes without emotion. Then he said: "I would suggest that the watch on Addington, and on Teebo, too, if it is possible, be doubled."

"Right," came the voice from the state department.

Benson hung up, then called police headquarters on a regular phone.

"Richard Benson talking. On the murder of Frank Teebo at the Coyle Hotel."

"Yes, sir," was the response. "What can we tell you about that?"

"Two people in the foyer of the Pink Room saw Teebo at the open window, though neither saw him actually fall. At any rate, that's their story."

"That's right. There was a woman in a white evening dress who gave her name as Emily Brace. A man in white tie and tails was with her. Name, Richard Addington."

"Have you followed them up?"

"No, sir. They seemed innocent enough. Just witnesses—and not important ones, either."

"Do you have their addresses?"

"We have the ones they gave. There seemed no reason to check them. If they're people who ought to have been held, it's possible the addresses are phonies. However, here they are—" He gave Dick the addresses.

"Thank you."

"Did we slip, Mr. Benson?" asked the police voice. "Should we have hauled the pair in?"

"I don't know, yet," said Benson evenly. "I'd like a free hand on these two, if you don't mind. I'll report later, if I find anything."

He turned from the phone and handed Smitty a slip of paper.

"Smitty, see if Richard Addington is at this address. If he is—"

"If he is," said the giant, doubling his vast fists, "I'll

104

try to keep from breaking his back in my two hands. I'll try to bring him in alive."

He went out.

Benson motioned to Nellie, and they went out, too, a few minutes later.

CHAPTER XI

Contact

It was Mac who noticed the birdhouse as he and Cole and Jessica Marsden drove in the gateway of the Marsden estate and up to the house.

It was a mansion of a birdhouse; but it wasn't open for tenants, it appeared.

From the front step, before Jessica had opened the big door, Mac pointed.

"That is cerrrtainly," he burred, "a hotel of a bird-house."

It sure was. It was as big as a wardrobe trunk.

Jessica smiled a little in spite of her distress at her father's desperate danger.

"Dad made it himself," she said. "We have kept some of the migrating birds here all winter by feeding them and letting them nest in the loft of the carriage house. Then they move out to that house in the spring."

"But not this spring," Mac pointed out. "Because it's all closed up. Funny it wasn't opened."

The girl stared. "That is funny," she said. "It was open two weeks ago. I remember distinctly. But now that it is pointed out, I don't remember having seen birds around it for some days."

She had the door open, now. And clearly, distinctly, the three could hear the hall phone ringing.

Jess turned a face that was white toward Cole Wilson. He nodded.

"That may be the gang, wanting to contact you about your father."

The two of them ran down the hall to the phone.

Mac did not follow them. He went to the giant tree in whose branches was the large birdhouse. There was a lower limb which he could just reach with a full jump upward. He got his bony hands over the limb and drew himself up like a circus acrobat.

In the hall, Jess grasped the phone like a drowning girl clutching at a life preserver.

"J-Jessica Marsden speaking," she said.

The hunch had been correct. This was the call they'd come here for.

"Where have you been?" snarled a man's voice. "Don't you care if your father lives or not?"

"I c-care very much!"

"All right, then listen. And get this straight. Your old man is O.K., now. He won't be if you don't do as we say. We want that picture called 'The Princess.' Bring us that, and we'll let your father go home with you. We'll even let him take the picture back with him. We don't want the thing, we just want to look at it and see if it is really a Vernier."

Jessica's shoulders slumped. Cole put an arm around them, in a purely brotherly way of course, to give her support. This was what Jess had known would happen, and what she had feared.

"Believe me when I say this," she declared. "I don't know where that picture is. Dad never told me. I can't get it for you."

"You're lying. Anyhow, you'd better be lying."

"I tell you, I don't know. Listen. Get my father to tell you where it is. Then you tell me. I'll get it for you, I swear; and I'll bring it wherever—"

"Yeah!" barked the man. "You think we haven't tried to make your father talk?"

"What have you done to him?" screamed Jess.

"Now, now, calm down. We didn't do much. But he . . . he's kind of asleep now. And he won't . . . er . . . wake up for maybe some hours. We can't wait that long. You get that picture and bring it to Grayson Cemetery in exactly an hour and a half."

"They've tortured him into unconsciousness," Jessica moaned to Cole, with her hand over the transmitter so her voice wouldn't carry. Then she spoke into the phone again. "I simply don't know where the picture is."

"O.K.," said the man on the other end of the line with a cold finality. "Then it's all up with your father. So long."

MacMurdie came in at just this moment. He had a long metal cylinder in his hand. "Got it!" he said.

"Oh, thank Heaven!" Jess clutched the phone. "Wait, whoever you are. Please wait! I can get the picture. I'll bring it to you."

There was so long a silence that she thought the man had hung up before hearing. But then he said: "Right. Hour and a half, Grayson Cemetery. And no tricks!"

Then he did hang up, and Jess and Cole turned to Mac.

The thing he had found in the birdhouse was a metal map case, of the type that could be hermetically sealed to protect valuable charts against weather. It was perfect to protect something else against weather, out there in a birdhouse where rain couldn't come in but dampness could.

The rolled canvas in the metal map case was the wanted picture, all right. "The Princess," in all its glowing colors and beautiful lines.

They stared at it. A beautiful thing, yes; but it had more than beauty. Somehow, in its interrelation of lines and colors, there was a deadly message. If they took it, the real picture, to the cemetery to get Jessica's father, and if the gang outwitted them and got hold of the painting, none knew what catastrophe would follow. And it would be their fault.

"We'll have to risk it," said Cole soberly.

Mac nodded. "You let me carry this case," he said.

Cole didn't reply. He had his little belt radio out and was trying to contact The Avenger. He wanted to report that the picture had been found and that contact was to be made in an hour and a half.

But he couldn't seem to get Benson with the call signal.

Emily Brace's home was less than nine miles from Bleek Street. That is, if it was her home—and not just a fake number.

But it was bona fide. The name stared at them from a card over a bell.

Benson rang the buzzer. There was no answer.

"Out," commented Nellie. She looked around at the modest vestibule. "This isn't an expensive building. Probably she has a job, living in a place like this, and is out working, now."

The Avenger said nothing. He started up the stairs— it was a walk-up building—with Nellie beside him.

They passed a door on the second landing where a radio was blaring.

Nellie grimaced. They could still hear the thing after starting up the third flight of stairs. This was that kind of building; you didn't need a radio yourself, you could hear

110

at least six through walls and doors at any moment of the day or evening.

Dick stopped as if he had run into a wall. So did Nellie. They listened to the news item from the blaring radio, then stared at each other.

"Late flash. A Brooklyn power plant, supplying current to thousands of homes and dozens of Brooklyn factories which are working on day-and-night shifts with defense orders, has just been disabled by a boiler explosion. At least, special police insist that the plant was wrecked by a boiler explosion. No evidence has yet been unearthed that it might have been sabotage—"

"The 'Diabolo,'" breathed Nellie. "They got it just in time to receive its instructions. In only a few hours that power plant has been ruined."

Benson nodded, his eyes like icy pools.

They went on to Emily Brace's door on the fourth floor. There was one more flight of steps above them; the building was five stories high.

The Avenger opened the door with a key formed from one of his plastic blanks. He stood a moment on the threshold, then shut the door behind him with a grim hand.

Nellie said: "Good heavens!"

Emily Brace was not working on some job. She was here. But she hadn't heard them ring. She would never hear anything anymore.

She was dead!

Dick Benson and Nellie bent gently down over the dead woman. She looked appealingly attractive, even in death. She had been shot in the back, and there was no anguish or strain on her face. It was as peaceful as if she were merely asleep.

111

She was still warm, so her death had been very recent. Another hint of time of death was that she was in a negligée, as though getting ready to go out for the evening. And this was just about the time for such dressing.

"She doesn't look like a criminal," said Nellie. "And this isn't a criminal's room. It's a place lived in by an average, decent person who made her own living and asked nothing of anyone. You can fairly feel that."

The Avenger didn't work on hunches. He preferred cold logic. But in this case he nodded agreement.

"I think she had nothing to do with this," he said. "I think she was the proverbial innocent bystander. On the night she was with Richard Addington, she learned something—or had a chance to learn something—that was dangerous to him. So he killed her."

"In that case we're too late and there's nothing to learn here—" Nellie began.

But The Avenger was acting as if there were plenty to learn. His pale eyes were searching over the room like twin microscopes.

"Perhaps she felt her danger," he mused, more to himself than to Nellie. "She may have left some word for—"

He was looking for articles not quite exactly in place. He saw that a little powder on the dressing case had spilled from a large box. He opened the box and explored. But there was nothing in the box but powder.

A lampshade was slightly crooked. He examined the lamp, standard, base and shade. Nothing concealed there. He opened a door and saw a dressing room with a bureau. On the bureau was a picture.

It showed a sleek, dark, rather good-looking man with a playboy's face, but with strength around the jaw.

Richard Addington.

But that was not the important thing. The thing was that the picture was not quite straight in the frame.

Benson took the picture out of the frame, and then his

colorless, infallible eyes glowed glacially. There was a long strip of paper in the backing, folded a half dozen times. And there was a sheet of note paper.

He came back out of the dressing closet with these, and Nellie read with him over his shoulder:

In case anything happens to me, investigate Richard Addington, of whom this is a photograph. I am sure he is a criminal of some sort, though I still cannot guess what he does. The color chart is also important, though I don't know why. I only know that my life has been in danger since—

That was all there was to it. The words ended in a sprawl of pencil. The note had been hastily put behind the photograph before being completed.

The Avenger unfolded the strip of paper and found that this was the mentioned color chart. The strip was about four feet long, and on it were fifty or sixty colors in little shiny oblongs. It was like the color chart every painter carries, except that Dick had never seen such a chart all in one row on a long strip of paper before. Usually, they are on big oblong cards in five or six rows.

"Emily Brace was right," said Benson. "How right, she never knew. This is important—"

"Quite," came a cultured, even voice from the window. "So important that lives mean nothing in comparison. Don't move, either of you."

Nellie could see the window by turning her head. She saw a man coming through. The man was Richard Addington!

Addington's weapon did not match his sleek appearance and his cultured voice. The weapon was a sawed-off shotgun, about the deadliest thing there is at short range. This was leveled at The Avenger and Nellie in such a

113

way that both would have died if the two barrels were discharged.

Addington stood beside the window, and Nellie saw a rope dangling.

Three more men came in, one after another. The window was four floors up, with nothing under it, so Benson and Nellie had paid it too little attention. The penalty was this soundless invasion from the rooftop.

The four came slowly toward Nellie and Benson. They stopped well out of reach, however, so there was no possibility of The Avenger grabbing one of them as a shield.

"I'll have that color chart," said Addington.

Nellie wondered why he simply hadn't let loose with both barrels of the shotgun, and then taken the chart from Dick's dead body. But glancing sideways at The Avenger, she got the grisly answer.

Dick had thought of that, too. He held the color chart next to his cheek. If Addington pulled the trigger, he would blow the chart as well as Benson's head into tatters.

"The chart," said Addington more sharply. "Drop it."

The Avenger didn't move.

Addington smiled. "One of you men," he said to his friends, "approach him from the side and get the chart."

They were all waiting for The Avenger to try something when this man was in reach. They were so sure that would be the moment when he'd try resistance that they didn't notice a slight move he made just as the men started their catlike advance.

The move was simply to press his right arm hard against his body.

Every suit The Avenger owned had a dozen or more intricate gadgets concealed in it. In this one, at the armpit, was a little sac with a tube running down to his wrist. The sac held a concentrated, inky vapor. When it was

114

squeezed and with the tube nozzle opened by the twitch of a finger at the same time, the vapor poured forth and instantly expanded.

It did so now!

The man had taken two steps for the chart when the room suddenly hazed.

There were yells. "Give it to him! Kill him!" And Richard Addington's crisp reply: "I can't blow that chart to pieces."

Then there was a rush for Nellie and Dick Benson. And that was a mistake, because there were only four of the men.

The Avenger found a throat with his steely fingers. He pressed at a section at the base of the skull. The man fought frantically for thirty seconds and then slumped. The anaesthetizing pressure on the big nerve center would keep him out for some minutes.

There was a thud as Nellie found someone in the black pall and threw him.

Then there was an unforeseen disturbance that testified to Addington's cautious generalship. Just as he'd done at Vaughan's penthouse, he had split his forces here and made entrance from two directions.

There were voices in the hall. Many voices. "Look at the smoke coming out the door crack! Bust in!"

Nellie felt a light hand on her arm. The hand pressed the code. "It's me." She went where the hand urged. Benson led to the window.

You still couldn't see an inch in the room. Behind them, there were still furious sounds, as the three men left conscious fought among themselves, thinking they had hold of the enemy. But already the door was opening; Nellie and The Avenger couldn't take on an army.

Nellie reached out the window and found the rope. She went up it with trained skill, and felt the rope tighten as The Avenger came, too. Then they were on the rooftop.

"They've caught on," she said, at the sound of shouts below. She twitched the rope up so none could follow that way. Then they ran for the next roof and a fire escape.

The Avenger's face was still like a mask, but Nellie knew this man as few others knew him; and in the expressionlessness, she could read a faint trace of emotion. It was that of cold fury, of defeat. So then she caught on.

"You saw that rope end when it first hung down," she accused. "You knew the men were coming. You let them come, in order to capture them."

"I didn't know they were coming," said The Avenger, tone calm and cool as his eyes. "But it seemed probable that we would have visitors. You see, it looked as though Emily Brace had been shot from a long distance, through the window, by a rifle equipped with telescopic sights. Otherwise, if she had been killed by someone in the room, there'd have been signs of a search; it was obvious that the color chart, which she'd somehow gotten hold of, was what the killers wanted. If she were killed from a distance, then men would be on the way to visit her apartment. As you say, I let them come, hoping to take them prisoner."

The cold fury glinted just once in the glacial, pale eyes again.

"Well," said Benson, "we didn't get them. But they didn't get the color chart, either. So we're even."

It was then that Cole finally got The Avenger's attention on the belt radio.

"Chief," came Cole's tiny voice through the set. "I've been trying to get you. There's important news. We have the picture, and the gang that holds Marsden has con-

116

tacted us. We are to take the picture to Grayson Cemetery in—" There was a pause as Cole calculated time elapsed from the moment when they'd been told to show up in an hour and a half. "In an hour and ten minutes," he said.

"Right," Dick said evenly. "We'll be there."

They were in the car now. Benson had pointed its nose for Bleek Street. Now, he turned and headed toward Long Island.

It was too bad he did so, because hell was popping at Bleek Street—a kind the pale-eyed man would have given a leg rather than miss.

CHAPTER XII

The Mark of Cain

"No tricks," the man had warned Jessica Marsden over the phone. The gang would be watching for trouble, so Jessica would have to meet them alone. They wouldn't approach her if a couple of men appeared along with her.

So two miles from Grayson Cemetery, which was about ten miles from the Marsden home, Cole and Mac got out of the girl's car.

Scared but game, she went on alone, with the metal map case containing the picture. Cole and Mac finished the trip on foot, coming up to the back of the block-square graveyard.

The cemetery was an old one, filled up long ago. Now, the only activity in connection with it was to keep it up. Consequently, after dark, at least, there wasn't a soul around.

And it was dark, now. There was no moon, and only a few stars showed weakly through baleful-looking clouds.

"Wonder where the skurlies will be lurkin'?" said Mac.

119

"Probably there'll be only one man hiding among the tombstones," guessed Cole. "He can give a signal if all's well, and the rest can come in with Marsden to trade for the painting."

"If they come with Marsden," retorted Mac, with all his Scotch pessimism, cropping up, "maybe they'll just take the picture and keep on holdin' the mon."

"Why would they do that?" shrugged Cole. "A gang of regular kidnappers might take payment and refuse to turn their victim free, because they'd want more payment in the future. But all this crew wants is that painting. They'd have no reason to keep Marsden after getting it."

There was a big tree within the cemetery, flinging a branch over the high, spike fence. Cole and Mac got up on this branch, then crawled along it and another branch till they were ten feet inside the grounds. But stayed up there for the moment.

Cole got out a pair of night glasses. The lenses were ground to The Avenger's formula to gather the maximum luminosity in darkness.

Even with these, Cole couldn't see much; but he saw enough to whisper an exclamation after a moment.

"There's Jess," he said to Mac. "She's coming up the drive in the car. The gang must have left the gate open. Now the gate closes. Jess stops—"

Mac, without glasses, could see the girl get out of the car because of her white dress.

Cole whispered:

"There's a man beyond the car, in the doorway of that biggest mausoleum, watching. Just one man, as far as I can make out."

There was a tiny flash of light. Mac saw the dim white blur which was Jessica's dress, as she went obediently toward the flash. Then the ray of light shot straight up against a tree, lasting for about a second.

"Signal to the others that everything's all right," Cole hazarded. "Yes, I can see a car, now, outside the fence toward the south, there. Two cars. They were ready to scram out of here if they had to, but now they feel they don't have to. There's a small side gate, just big enough for pedestrians, not for cars. It's open. They're coming in—"

"Give me those glasses for a change," rasped Mac, "instead of givin' me this blow-by-blow description. What do ye think ye are, a radio announcer?"

He grabbed the night glasses. He saw six men stealing toward the central mausoleum. One of the men seemed to be in such a daze that he could hardly walk. He held his arms stiffly beside him.

"They're bringin' Marsden all right," said Mac. "They have his arms tied. We'd better join them, Cole."

The two dropped noiselessly from the tree. The marvelous little night glasses had shown no one lurking around the north half of the cemetery, so they went down that side of the central drive.

Probably no one but another member of Justice, Inc., could have perceived their expert approach. And even Smitty or Nellie or The Avenger would have had to be looking right at them to spot them.

They slid from gravestone to gravestone, two faint shadows in a world of shadows, without sound. Over their faces were black squares of cloth, to keep the lights of their skin from showing. Over their hands were black gloves.

They got to a square shaft within twenty feet of the mausoleum doorway. There, they could see and hear quite well.

"Got it, huh?" said the man in the doorway. They could not see his face, but they could see that he was enormously fat. In the dimness, there seemed no end to the spread of the man.

"Yes," said Jessica in a low tone. She extended the cylindrical, metal case. "Where is my father?"

121

"He'll be along. I want a look at this."

There was a click as the fat man opened the case. There was another flash as he rayed his small light over the painting, making sure that it was the one the gang was after.

"O.K.," he sais huskily. "This is 'The Princess,' all right. You showed good sense in not trying to trick us." He raised his voice a little. "Bring Marsden."

Jessica whirled with a suppressed cry at the sound of shuffling feet. Obviously, she hadn't known till then that she was not alone here with the fat man, though, of course, Cole and Mac were presumably not too far away.

The five men who came up to the mausoleum were almost carrying the sixth.

"Dad," cried Jessica, "what have they done to you?"

"Shut up!" snarled the fat man. "He's all right."

Jessica had her arms around her father. He reeled there.

"You can take the gag off in ten minutes," said the fat man. "Stay here for that length of time, too. Then you can do anything you please."

Cole tensed beside Mac, feeling that their moment had come. They ought to get the picture back, now that the girl had her father and the gang their painting. Moreover, they ought to try to capture that crew. It was six men against two, but The Avenger's aides had faced heavier odds than that.

They took a few noiseless steps after the gang, then stopped in amazement.

So did the gang.

A voice had sounded, eerie, faint but clear, where no voice had any right to exist.

Inside the shuttered mausoleum.

"The mark of Cain," sighed the voice. "On your forehead is the mark of Cain."

There was a moment of stunned silence on the part of all. Then the fat man spoke.

"What . . . was that?" He sounded as if he'd been running and was badly out of breath.

"On your forehead," came the weird, faint voice in direct answer, "is hell's mark. The mark of Cain."

The fat man dropped the map case. He was trembling violently. Another man, whose face couldn't be seen in the darkness, picked the case up.

"Look here," panted the fat man to his fellows. "I was told . . . a frame-up— What does that voice mean?"

It didn't mean a thing to Cole and Mac, except as a puzzling and rather scary hint that maybe, after all, there was such a thing as a ghost. But it obviously meant a great deal to the fat man. He was becoming more frightened by the minute.

"Aw, come on," grated the man who had picked up the cylindrical metal container. "Whatever this is, we haven't time to monkey around."

Jessica had kept her head. She wasn't in sight now. She'd taken her father to the car. They heard the door slam and her motor start. She'd taken full advantage of the distraction.

Mac and Cole crouched for a rush. But then the man who had picked up the map case gave a yell.

"It's a trick! Stop that girl! Kill Marsden!"

Cole, wondering, saw that he'd taken the painting out of the case once more—and saw in the dimness that it didn't look like a picture any more.

It looked vaguely like a lace tablecloth.

Then Cole couldn't see it any more because the man dropped it as if it had burned him.

"It's a trap! Get away!"

Cole and Mac were rushing the crew. They saw one man raise his hand. In it was a thing like a small pineapple, and they threw themselves to the ground. It was a bomb!

But the man never threw it.

123

There was a *phhht* of sound, and the man fell with a shallow gash on the top of his head.

"The chief!" said Mac.

The Avenger's tiny gun, Mike, had made that deadly whisper. And it had spat a slug with Dick's inimitable accuracy, so that it creased the man; glanced off the top of his skull and knocked him unconscious, instead of killing him.

The mausoleum door swung open and two dim shapes came out. The Avenger and Nellie.

They started after the remaining five men along with Mac and Cole. But the capture of the gang was not to take place. The yell of the man with the map case had come just an instant too soon.

The five were retreating. And two of them had belching submachine guns in their hands. Bullets sprayed in a deadly arc in front of them as they went. Corners chipped from marble slabs; whines sounded as slugs ricocheted.

The four went after them from shelter to shelter. But they were beaten. They saw the gang get back through the side gate and rushed as car doors thudded shut.

The Avenger's arm snapped forward in an expert throw. There was an explosion, and the rear end of one of the cars jumped. But the grenade didn't disable the machine. The cars whirled off.

"Domn!" groaned Mac.

The Avenger's pale eyes swung his way. So did Nellie's and Coles.

" 'Tis my fault the skurlies got away," said Mac. "If I'd known ye'd set a trap for them—"

"I don't get it," said Cole.

"The picture," Mac moaned. "I put sulphuric acid in that case before givin' it to the girl. It burned the paintin' to shreds."

"Oh!" said Nellie.

"Yes. So the picture was all right when the fat man looked at it. But then that other skurlie had to look at it again, a few minutes later, and be warned somethin' was wrong. So they got away. I'm sorry, chief. I didn't know ye'd be at our elbows."

"Nellie and I have been in the mausoleum for a quarter of an hour. We simply entered it as a hiding place; but then the man chanced to pick it as a meeting spot, probably because it's central and the biggest structure here. So I tried to unnerve him a bit with a ghostly whisper before attacking."

"Ye unnerved him, all rrright," burred Mac. "Ye unnerrrved me, too. What was all that about the mark of Cain?"

But Benson didn't answer. He turned to Cole. "Miss Marsden?"

"She was to go with her father to Bleek Street. She'll probably get there about the time we do."

"Anyhow," said Nellie, looking regretfully in the direction in which the gang had escaped, "they haven't that picture to work on."

"And we have at least one of the gang on ice," nodded Mac. "The one Muster Benson creased with Mike. I'll get him."

He came back through the side gate in a moment with the unconscious man over his shoulder. They went to where Benson had hidden his car, and then rolled back to Bleek Street.

And there, with midnight not far off, they got their next bad jolt.

Smitty and Josh and Rosabel were up in the big top-floor room. Smitty was swearing steadily, and his face was white. Josh and Rosabel were doing nothing.

They were lying on the floor, and the giant was working frantically over them.

The Avenger's icy, pale eyes went from them to Smitty.

"I think they're dead," said Smitty in anguish. "Somebody poisoned them or something. I came in from look-

125

ing up Addington's supposed address on Gramercy Park and found Josh and Rosabel on the stairs just inside the vestibule door. The painting, 'The Dock,' was unrolled beside them."

"If they've killed these two—" began Cole, through set teeth.

But then Josh moaned a little, and his eyes opened. He looked at Dick, who was now bending over Rosabel.

"She . . . all right?" whispered Josh. Rosabel was the core of his life; the two were a devoted couple. So his first inquiry was about her.

Benson, finger on her pulse, which was improving, nodded. Josh relaxed, and a faint, bitter laugh came from his lips.

"I . . . thought I was smart," he whispered. "The buzzer rang. The screen showed one man in the vestibule. This dark one, Addington. He offered a hundred thousand dollars for a look at the picture. Just a look. So Rosabel and I thought we'd trap him."

Even at such a moment, Mac grinned a bit. The bribe was funny, if Addington had known it. If there was anything that did not interest any of Justice, Inc., it was an offer of money. The Avenger, though few knew it, was one of the richest men in existence; and what he had all his aides could share any time.

"We said we'd bring the picture to the vestibule and he could look at it there. We meant to get him just inside; then he'd be all through."

Josh didn't have to explain. All could grasp his plan. The bottom half of the stairs, on the first level, could be closed off at the press of a button, so that whoever was on them would be trapped in a steel box. Rosabel and Josh had meant thus to trap Addington.

"We went down and showed the picture through the glass of the inner vestibule door to Addington," Josh went on weakly. "We said he'd better step in on the stairs where the light was better. He did. Rosabel, behind me,

126

reached for the trap button. And then we went down."

Josh looked as if he could break down and bawl.

"There was a flower in his buttonhole. There must have been a little squirter in it, some gas. Anyway, I didn't remember anything after that till now, when I woke up to see you all here."

"You had 'The Dock,' you say?"

"Yes." Josh shivered. He needed no one to point out the full meaning of this. "Addington had plenty of time to go over it. And it's been over an hour now, since he left."

They were all grimly silent at that.

Whatever message of chaos and death lay in "The Dock," had by now been deciphered. It was the worst defeat of all.

The buzzer sounded. Josh reeled to the television screen with forlorn hope in his eyes that maybe it was Addington again, indiscreetly visiting, for one last time, the headquarters of his enemy.

But it wasn't, of course.

"Miss Marsden and her father," Josh sighed.

"Put them up in a suite on the second floor," said The Avenger, voice metallic.

Then he stepped to the limp form of the hoodlum they had brought from the cemetery.

CHAPTER XIII

Investment in Death

"The address Addington gave the cops was a phony," said Smitty. "There is no such address on Gramercy Park."

The Avenger only nodded. It would have been remarkable if the address had not been a fake one.

Meanwhile, he was going through the captured gunman's personal effects. And he found something in the lining of his coat.

If that strip of paper had not been so carefully concealed in the man's coat lining, even the infallible eyes of The Avenger might not have caught its significance, because it certainly didn't look important.

It was a strip about four feet long and two or three inches wide, of the kind of paper on rolls that banks use in adding up figures for a monthly statement. On the strip, there appeared to be a long list of someone's stock holdings.

Such things as U.S. Steel, Amer. Can., Tel. and Tel., with the current prices after each.

129

But that strip was, at a glance, about the same length as the strip on which was the color chart, which The Avenger had taken from Emily Brace's apartment. And when it was laid next to the color chart, it could be seen that the stock quotations were so spaced as to coincide exactly with a strip of color, apiece.

Benson's eyes were like chips of ice as he unrolled "The Dock" and thumbtacked it to his desk top.

"Get the ruler we took from the blond man, Harris," he said evenly.

Cole got it and took it to him. All crowded around, perceiving that something momentous was up.

The Avenger turned the ruler so that its back, with the single mark on it, was up. He measured off that space from the right-hand side of the painting and put a tiny dot there. Then he laid the ruler down so that the upper side was revealed, with the bottom end exactly at the dot. As he moved, he spoke evenly, his calm voice revealing no more emotion than his expressionless face.

"We know a great deal about all this, now. There is a ring of picture thieves, with some members in France and some in this country. The French members smuggle out looted masterpieces in some cases. In others, where they can't get the originals, they have a clever copyist turn out fakes."

He was marking the points at which the lines on the ruler came on the painting. All saw where the top line came. It coincided with the little fisher boy's red nose.

"Behind that gang of ordinary crooks, not even suspected by the crooks, is a subtle crew of spies and saboteurs with official connections. The first gang is allowed to smuggle these paintings out, though they don't know that. But before the pictures go out, they are charted for certain colors to be matched later on one of these strips. If the colors wanted can't be found in an original painting, they either touch up one of the tints, as was done on

130

'Diabolo,' or put out a copy with the right tints as was done with 'The Dock.' "

Dick was matching the colors on the painting, marked by the odd ruler, with the colors on the chart.

"This second gang permits the pictures to be brought to this country and sold. If any trouble arises, the police will arrest what seems to be an ordinary gang of criminals in a fake-masterpiece racket and won't bother to investigate further. But, as each picture is sold, the second gang traces it down, gets access to it long enough to decipher the message with a color chart and strip of paper like this one, then follows the instructions so given.

"The home office of a foreign intelligence bureau, with nation-wide reports on the head man's desk, would know better than any saboteur which dams, plants, ships were key objects to be destroyed. This would be the reason why orders came from a distance—via pictures—not only as to when to destroy an object but also as to what to undermine in the first place.

"The way the enemy has it worked out, the timing of the sabotage acts is the important part of the plan. In earlier pictures, instructions were given as to what to prepare for destruction. In later ones, saboteurs were told just when to push the button, with the catastrophe to come at just the worst moment for United States morale. The timing of destructive blows can be more demoralizing than the destruction itself.

"This time element is also the reason why the saboteurs needed so little time to look at the later pictures in order to decipher instructions. They already knew what object to destroy, and they needed only the time it would take them to learn when to act. Sometimes there is trouble. They'd have had a hard time getting to 'The Dock' if it were here in Bleek Street. This place is like a fortress. So Addington promptly killed Teebo at the Pink Room to prevent such a sale. We got 'The Dock' anyhow; and they had to take desperate risks to get at it for the

131

required few minutes, which they succeeded in doing."

"How do you suppose Addington managed the Pink Room murder?" Nellie asked.

The Avenger's shoulders moved in a slight shrug.

"Probably used a silenced gun. The force of the slug would topple Teebo forward out the window. Perhaps Emily Brace later began to connect that death with some sound like a slap—the gun—which she remembered hearing. That would make it necessary for Addington to murder her. That and the fact that she'd gotten hold of one of the color charts."

"But you're forgetting that we've since seen Teebo, this man supposed to be murdered," objected Smitty.

The Avenger didn't answer. He was laying the color chart beside the strip of paper. On the chart was marked each shade of color noted by a ruler marking.

Mac shook his dour head as he watched. "I got it. The numbers and letters marked by the different shades should spell a message. But would all those paper strips be the same? Maybe this strip goes with 'The Princess,' Marsden's picture, which has been destroyed?"

"Maybe it does," nodded Benson, pale eyes intent. "But I'm hoping either that all the strips are the same—the color charts are undoubtedly all the same—or that this is the strip that goes with this painting. After all, they didn't get to it till just a short time ago—"

He marked down on separate paper the letters and numbers coinciding with the marked shades on the color chart.

"They're a clever crew, all right. No suspected foreign agent, watched constantly by our government operatives, could get in a code message that wouldn't be intercepted and read. But through another gang, which itself doesn't even know how they're being used, Addington and his band have time and again deciphered full instructions from pictures. Their color charts and paper strips would mean nothing to an observer. The pictures would mean nothing. But put them together, and—"

He stopped, and flashed to his feet. He stared at the words and figures he had finished marking as if at a poisonous snake. His face was still its usual masklike self, but on his forehead the rest saw moisture suddenly appear.

"This gives a message all right. Listen:

"'U.S. Zinc 8¼. Carolina Chemical 19. Philadelphia Die Casting 3½. Gas Products 45.'"

Nellie stared in bewilderment at The Avenger, and then up at gigantic Smitty, who looked equally bewildered.

"If that's a message, I'm a gor—" began Smitty.

But there was to be no time for talk.

"All of us," snapped Benson. "To the hangar. The amphibian. Mac, you and Cole gather up diving helmets for three. Hurry!"

The secret hangar of Justice, Inc., was a dilapidated and apparently disused dock on the East River. At least, that was where the amphibians were kept.

The little band got there in double-quick time; and, still mystified, Cole Wilson piled aboard three sets of diving apparatus. Then they were in the air and winging south and west—Nellie and Smitty, Mac, Cole and Dick.

Nellie said, "What is all this, chief? Can you explain, now?"

The Avenger nodded patiently. He set the robot control, and drew out the paper. They looked again at the seemingly senseless list.

U.S. Zinc 8¼.

Carolina Chemical 19.

Philadelphia Die Casting 3½.

Gas Products 45.

"Carolina and Philadelphia," said Benson. "How do they tie together?"

"They don't," said Nellie.

But Mac, eyes suddenly narrowed, said: "There's a big navy yard at Philadelphia. In the yard is one of our newest battleships, the *Carolina*."

"Right. And what can happen to ships?"

"They can sink."

"Hey!" said Smitty. "Zinc—sink. I get it!"

"So we have, 'Sink (battleship) *Carolina* (at) Philadelphia (navy yard). Now for the numbers. 8¼ 19 3½ 45. The fractions are only window dressing to make the stock quotation prices look authentic. These quotations are nowhere near correct, by the way, for the stocks listed. So we take out the fractions. We get 8 19 3 45. Date, and hour for action. August 19th, 3:45 P.M. or A.M.?—almost certainly A.M. An attempt at sabotage could be made much more easily in the pitch darkness of 3:45 in the morning than in the broad daylight of afternoon. So there's the message."

"My gosh!" exploded Smitty. " 'Sink battleship *Carolina* at the Philadelphia Navy Yard at 3:45 on the morning of August 19th.' My gosh!"

"Exactly!" said The Avenger, looking at his watch. "And it is now one o'clock in the morning of August 19th!"

He took over the controls again and tried for another mile or two of speed as the plane winged toward Philadelphia.

"It's impossible," Nellie kept murmuring. "There's no way they could do a thing like that."

"There was no way to destroy the King Dam and powerhouse, the Lorenville, Indiana, powder mill, and the four ships at the Hoboken dock," retorted Cole. "But they did it. And they'll do this, too, if we can't stop them."

"We've got to stop them!" said Mac. "We can't let a battleship be blown up."

"There's more at stake even than the *Carolina*," said The Avenger. "This gang knows now that the painting racket is washed up. They'll never try that again. They'll disperse, after this job, till a new code system is worked up. Then they can start all over again on another round of sabotage. The fate of the country may depend not only on our stopping this act but also rounding up that bunch—Addington, Teebo and all."

"Teebo!" squawked Smitty. "But we saw—"

"Oh, stop it!" said Nellie. "Sure, we saw Teebo fall out a window. Or somebody else did. So what?"

"Wait a minute!" said Cole suddenly. "There's another point here. That last item. Gas Products. Was that used only to get the number, 45?"

"I think not," said Benson. "I think that has its place in this. There is a Gas Products Corporation in Philadelphia that does a large business supplying gas and oil to boats. It has a big dock off Camden. I believe that is to be used as a base."

He looked at Nellie and Smitty, and in his pale cold eyes was fear, the only kind of fear The Avenger knew, for the safety of his aides—never for himself.

"You two go to the Gas Products wharf," he said. "It's a nasty assignment. There may be thirty or forty men there who will stop at nothing. But the place has to be watched. On your way, you can tip off the Federal men to send a force to surround the place as soon as they can get a dozen or so operatives rounded up."

"Right," said Nellie, blue eyes glowing.

"Take care of yourselves," said Benson tensely. "And—good luck."

CHAPTER XIV

Ship of Doom

The battleship *Carolina,* moored at the navy yard, looked like something painted by a designer of mammoth stage sets.

The giant hull had slid down the ways months ago. Now hundreds of workmen were finishing the towering superstructure. It was a hive of activity.

Electric engines ran cars of material along the dock; electric cables and air hoses, like a multitude of snakes, ran from compressors and power plants to the boat. Bathing the whole thing was a glare of lights almost equalling the sun. Day and night, they were working on the ponderous floating fortress. Soon she'd be finished, a thirty-five-thousand-ton monster.

The commandant of the yard, a man with white hair and a strong, lined face, stared at this glaringly illuminated picture of activity, and then at The Avenger.

"I've heard of you, Mr. Benson," he said. "I know your reputation. Yet, I can't believe sabotage of the *Carolina*

137

could be attempted on a large scale. A small fire from thermite smuggled aboard, a cable shorted with a phonograph needle—that sort of thing, perhaps. But nothing really disastrous."

"I wish I could believe you were right," said Benson.

"Look how it's illuminated," argued the commandant. "And it's the same below decks. A rat couldn't sneak aboard. All the workmen have identification badges and are known by sight, besides, to their foremen. The foremen are tested men. So a saboteur couldn't slip aboard disguised as a toolmaker, machinist or electrician."

"There is one angle of attack you may have overlooked," Dick said.

He pointed at the water, lighted like a polished plate above—but dark and mysterious and unfathomable below.

The commandant smiled.

"We have sonic devices constantly on guard," he said. "No underwater craft could get close, and perhaps discharge divers with explosives, without our hearing the noise of the propeller."

"Nevertheless," said The Avenger, "my friends and I would like to do a bit of diving of our own. Where can we submerge near the hull so that we won't be noticed? We have self-contained oxygen units—air hose and pumps are not necessary."

Three men came up to the little group. Each had his hand on a gun butt.

"Oh, it's you, sir," said one of them, looking at the commandant. "These men are with you?"

"Yes." The men left. The commandant turned to Benson with a shrug. "You see? There are guards all through here. But if you want to look around below—"

He led the way to the end of the dock. Two gondolas on rails were there. In the shadow, out of sight of any of the men swarming near the *Carolina*'s massive bulk, Dick and Mac and Cole put on the diving helmets, adjusted the little oxygen tanks, and fixed lead weights.

They descended on steel rungs, down, down, into cold blackness. And was it black! The person who talks of "Pitch darkness" will never know what that means till he has gone into sixty feet of water in the dead of night.

In the icy ooze of the bottom, The Avenger turned back toward where the *Carolina* was berthed. He had counted three hundred and seventy steps from the bow of the battleship. He went slowly back three hundred and seventy steps, with Mac and Cole holding hands and trailing behind. Then they went another two hundred steps which should bring them well under the hull.

Mac thought he could fairly feel the colossal weight of the floating steelyard above him, but he knew this was imagination. Water pressure remains constant.

Cole's clutching fingers pressed code on Mac's wrist. "Now what?"

Mac tapped the code for a question mark. He didn't know, either.

Then the Scot felt The Avenger's arm tighten.

Dick's weighted feet had touched something that might have been a length of electric cable, fallen by accident from a workman's hands—or that might not be here by accident.

He bent and touched it with his hands. And he touched it very gently indeed. He began following it, with Cole and Mac still trailing and never losing physical contact with each other. If they ever got separated in this blackness—

"It must be about a quarter of three," Mac thought.

That meant they had an hour to work. Meanwhile, the dour Scot wondered where Benson was leading them. He hadn't felt that length of wire as The Avenger had.

Benson reached the end of the electric cable. Mac felt him stand as still as stone, and, now, The Avenger's arm under Mac's fingers was like a bar of iron.

139

Benson tapped to Mac: "Move forward. Very slowly. Feel very carefully."

Mac followed instructions. And then he felt his hair literally stand on end, and he struggled for breath as if some one had kicked him in the stomach.

His questing fingers touched metal containers.

There were large round drums and smaller square cans. They were in a compact mass, as though someone had erected a barrier of cans and drums. A wall of them.

The wall reached up as high as Mac could stretch, and there seemed no end to its thickness and length.

Explosive! Tons of the stuff! Carried here slowly and laboriously; piled up night after night for no guessing how long.

So they had sonic detectors at the yard? Maybe. But, somehow, Addington's gang had worked around the detectors.

There was enough stuff here to blow half the bottom out of the *Carolina!* If it were touched off, it would take many months to repair the damage. Many months, and many millions of dollars.

But it would be worse in its general effect on the morale of the country. The nerve of the man in the street would be battered as badly as the giant ship.

"So they can sneak right into a navy yard and blow up a battleship, huh? Say, if they can do that any time they want to, what a pushover we'd be in a real war!"

A nation can't fight with ideas like that prevailing.

Mac started to tell Cole about this with rapid finger pressures. But suddenly Cole's hand wasn't there.

Cole wished fervently that it was!

He had known that something momentous was up, as he stood just behind The Avenger and Mac, but he knew better than to press forward to investigate without instructions. Then Mac had touched him with his other hand.

Anyhow, it had felt like that.

The Scot's left hand was extended backward, in Cole's light grip. But Cole felt a touch at his right hand. It felt like a fish at first, but then he made out fingers.

He started to tap a question, and the fingers of this extra hand tightened and he was yanked back in the inky blackness!

His loose grasp on Mac's hand was torn free before he could tighten his fingers. He lunged forward against the unexpected pull, trying to reach Mac and warn him. But he couldn't stretch that far.

He was still hauled backward as if at the end of a steel cable. He writhed and groped for whatever was tugging at him. He felt arms, shoulders. Then he felt something else—the sharp sting of a needle jabbing his arm.

In the blackness around him, Cole thought he saw colored flares suddenly burst, though this was ridiculous down in sixty feet of water. Then he wasn't wondering about the flares any more—or about anything else.

He was all through.

Mac was trying to reach Cole, during this time, and still keep contact with Benson. The Scot's arm searched hastily in the blackness.

"The mon's insane," he told himself, inside his helmet. "Leavin' loose of me in this blackness. Doesn't he realize—"

Then Mac was yanked backward, too, just after he touched what he thought was Cole's figure. It came at a very bad moment. Mac, to reach back further for the erring Cole, had momentarily loosed his clutch on The Avenger's wrist, thinking this would be all right for just an instant if he didn't move from where he stood.

So, when Mac was drawn backward, The Avenger didn't even have the slight warning of slipping fingers that Mac had had. But Benson didn't need that warning.

141

Alert as a tiger, sensitive as a cello string, he had felt something wrong.

The water had whirled a little, giving much the sensation of a slight breath of air on a still day. Instantly, he groped backward. But he felt neither Mac nor Cole.

The Avenger stood very still. No need to think anything out; he knew instantly all about it. Men were still bringing more containers, more explosive, to add to the terrible pile. These men had touched Cole and Mac in the dark—and had captured them.

What then? Either death at once, sixty feet from the clean fresh air of night, or death later, in some unnameable place and manner.

It is possible that at that moment the face of The Avenger was for once not a mask, that it expressed as much emotion as though he were an ordinary person instead of a crime-fighting machine. For certainly his was a horrible choice.

He could try to locate his aides in the blackness and help them. Or he could ignore them and try to make the huge pile of explosive harmless, quite possibly failing, because if there was more than one detonating cable he could all too easily miss finding the spare in his blind groping in blackness.

The members of Justice, Inc., were not professional heroes. They did not take unnecessary risks just to enhance the glamour of their exploits.

The Avenger had told Smitty and Nellie to get in touch with the Federal investigators on their way to the wharf of Gas Products Corp. They'd have done this even without orders. The more of Uncle Sam's men they could get to help in this, the better they'd like it.

The first thing Smitty and Nellie did on hitting the Camden shore line—The Avenger and Mac and Cole went on to the navy yard—was hunt a phone.

But phones along the waterfront are scarce at two

o'clock in the morning. And Nellie and Smitty, as well as the rest, were racing desperately against time.

"There isn't a light for a mile," groaned Smitty. "And we're almost to Gas Products. See? Down the line two blocks."

A street light showed on the sign. Also a moment later, it showed a solitary figure swinging lithely along with an occasional whistle.

"Certainly cheerful for this time of night," said Nellie resentfully. Then she said, "Oh, it's a boy."

The young fellow, about sixteen, with a clean, boyish face, drew near them.

"Looks O.K.," said Smitty. "Hey!"

The boy came over to them. He looked alert and smart. Smitty liked his appearance. The giant swiftly decided to take a chance on him.

"Want to earn five bucks?" he said.

"Sure, if it's legal," said the boy promptly.

"It's legal. And how! Know where the F.B.I. office is in this town?"

"I sure do."

"Well, go there, fast, and tell them to rush a bunch of men—a lot of men—to the Gas Products wharf. Tell them it's on the advice of Richard Benson, of Justice, Inc. They'll know who that is."

It was apparent from the awe on the boy's face that he knew who that was, too.

"Gee!" he gulped. "B-Benson? The Avenger? I've read about him. I think I've read about you, too. The big fella. Smitty?"

"Correct," said the giant. "Beat it, kid!"

"I don't want money for this," said the boy, trying to give the five back.

"Keep it. On your way—fast."

"O.K. A bunch of Federal men at Gas Products wharf quick."

He pounded down the street at an excited run, a lithe, alert youngster.

But not alert enough to notice when two shadows detached themselves from the gloom of an areaway when Nellie and Smitty had turned their backs. One of the two shadows silently pursued the boy. The other went down the next areaway to approach Gas Products' vast wharf from the rear.

The first shadow caught the boy three blocks away. Without sound and without mercy, the man clubbed down with a blackjack! The boy fell, and lay like a dead thing—

Nellie and Smitty were in a hurry, but not in so much of a hurry as to barge right into their destination. There was no percentage in making such haste that they would be captured without having a chance to strike at their enemies.

So they stood in a dark warehouse doorway across the street from the Gas Products building and looked it over.

The building was immense, running out into the water and with, no doubt, a spacious wharf behind that.

"How do we get in this joint without waking everybody up?" mused Smitty.

Nellie's small white hand came to rest on his arm.

"The third floor," she said, "looks like the office part of the building. Anyhow, the second window from the end is open a foot."

Smitty nodded. "O.K. Fire escape to the roof, then lower ourselves to the window."

His hand went to his waist. Coiled there was thirty feet of cord, hardly thicker than heavy fishline but so strong that it would support even Smitty's weight. A tiny steel grappling hook went with this, and small cross bars to hang onto.

They started across the street.

"Wait a minute," said Nellie. "This place seems outwardly respectable, but it is probably secretly owned by the enemy. If there's a lookout, we don't want to walk right to the building. Let's go up the street, then sneak back."

They walked to the corner, swung close to the building wall and stole back again. They got to the fire escape.

Half a dozen men swarmed silently around the right-hand corner of the building and ran toward them. Half a dozen more rounded the left-hand corner.

"Of all the lousy luck," groaned Smitty.

But it wasn't too bad. His hands jammed into his pockets and came out with some of Mac's anaesthetic pellets. They could bowl over every man here in about twenty seconds.

"Oh!" said one of the men advancing toward them. He kept his voice low. "I get it. You're the two who sent the message. We thought you were part of the gang."

"Message?" said Smitty.

"To the bureau," said the man impatiently.

It was neatly done. And, besides, circumstances had combined to give the appearance of logic. About eight minutes had passed since Smitty had dispatched the boy.

"Say! You guys are sure fast," said Smitty. He put the pellets back in his pockets. "Your office must be right around the corner for the kid to get there so fast. And you guys must have been playing pinochle right in the office to—"

"Smitty!" Nellie yelled suddenly. "These men are not—"

They leaped, then. Smitty tried to get the pellets out again, but he was just too late. Guns jabbed him all over; Nellie, too.

"Their heads," snarled one of the men. "This gang wears bullet-proof underwear, or something."

That relaxed the giant's muscles, tensed for a fighting trust in the celluglass undergarments.

The gang herded them toward the door, into it, and down a flight of stairs. At every second the guns were

145

leveled at Nellie's blonde locks and at the giant's head. There was no chance to try for a break. They were hopelessly caught!

CHAPTER XV

Backfire!

The room was hardly larger than a clothes closet and was of solid steel. Its walls, curved at the side, were straight at front and back. Through the center of the room ran a pipe about eighteen inches in diameter, and the outside of the pipe was sweating.

Cole Wilson opened his eyes, closed them again, then snapped them open a second time and stared in bewilderment.

"What's all this?" he demanded.

Mac had been conscious for several minutes. He said: "We're in a submarine. The sub that brought the divers and the explosive."

There was silence. Cole listened hard. All he could hear was a faint hum like that of an electric fan.

"Say, this is a sweet boat," he exclaimed. "I can't hear a motor, can't even feel the throb of the propeller."

"I don't think there is a propeller," said Mac. "I think

a silent worm-gear pump forces water through that pipe, that runs the length of the sub. That pulls the sub along on a kind of cable of water. They'd get very little speed out of her, but she'd be so silent that the sound devices wouldn't give an alarm."

"Then she is a sweet boat!"

Even the faint hum ceased, now, and the two men sensed that the submarine was slowing. They had been out quite a while.

"Now what?" wondered Cole.

Mac shrugged as well as he could. Both men were bound so they could hardly move a finger.

"A bigger question," said the Scot, "is why we're alive at all? Why did this murrrderin' bunch take us alive and go to the trouble of bringing us into the sub through their air lock?"

"I think I can guess that," said Cole thoughtfully. "They want to know how much damage, if any, we did to their plan. They'll probably hold us till after the hour when the explosion is due. Then, if it doesn't come off, we'll be tortured into telling what we did to stop it, so they can fix it up."

A steel bulkhead door swung open and into the steel room came a man they had come to hate with everything in them. A man with dark, sleek hair and a face that looked like that of an amiable playboy—Richard Addington.

Behind him came four men.

"Up with them," said Addington, nodding to the bound two. "Take them to the basement. I understand they'll have company down there."

Mac and Cole were picked up, carried out of the submarine and along a dimly lit tunnel. The bearers didn't bother to keep them from scraping along the rough stone sides.

They were carried into a well-lighted, huge room, and they saw what was meant by "company."

"Smitty!" groaned Cole. "Nellie!"

The giant and the tiny blonde looked glumly back at them.

"So they got you, too," said Smitty.

Then he was silent. They were all silent, all prayerfully thinking the same thing: Just one of their number was free, now. That was The Avenger himself. But it was doubtful if he alone could do anything, back there in the darkness under the vast *Carolina,* to prevent this ruinous enemy act.

Mac hated to ask even this small favor of any of this crew. But he simply had to know.

"Would ye mind tellin' me the time?" he asked in the general direction of this modern pirate band.

Addington did the answering.

"I'd be very glad to tell you," he said, grinning balefully. "It is now twenty-five minutes of four."

Ten minutes till the explosion time. If there was an explosion. They clung to the hope that, somehow, The Avenger, single-handed, had managed to take the sting out of that pile of metal containers.

Then they had all hope knocked from them.

Two more men came in the doorway that led, through the tunnel, to the concealed underground slip where the electric submarine was moored.

With them, they had Dick Benson!

The Avenger was bound even more securely than his aides, for, by now, Addington's gang knew more about the pale-eyed man's deadliness and were taking no chances of his escape.

"Chief!" wailed Nellie.

One of the men said in answer to Addington's perplexed but triumphant expression: "The guy got too smart this time. You know what? He managed to follow us back in the blackness to the sub. He rode her here to the wharf. But there we got him. We saw him just after you'd carried these two out"—he nodded to Cole and Mac— "and we nailed him."

They dumped Benson down beside his aides. He sat there, back to the wall, not a big man, weighing no more than a hundred and sixty-five pounds, securely bound—and yet, still seeming dangerous.

His pale and terrible eyes sent their probing stare at first one and then another of the score of men in the basement. And they looked uneasy at its cold impact.

All but Addington. The dark, sleek man stepped to the bound crime fighter and prodded him with his toe.

"So for once," Addington said, "you come up against a force you can't beat, just as your country has. I suppose you think you have rendered our mine under the *Carolina* harmless?"

"I know I have," said Benson quietly.

Mac and Cole stared triumphantly at each other. Smitty and Nellie sighed contentedly. Then anything that happened to them personally was all right. They all knew they'd sooner or later be killed in their dangerous work. Now was as good a time as any, since they could go out knowing they'd done this important job for their country.

"I suppose you concentrated on the detonating cables?" said Addington.

"Yes," said The Avenger, "I found them all."

"In that undersea darkness?" said Addington incredulously. "You found three cables—not daring to use a light of any kind—and rendered all three useless?"

"I did," said The Avenger, voice as expressionless as his mask of a face.

"Oh, boy!" said Smitty.

Mac boomed. "So, ye skurlies—" Then he stopped. Because Addington wasn't looking as downcast as he should.

In fact, Addington was beginning to laugh. He rocked with laughter.

"I said you'd met a force you couldn't beat," he exulted finally. "There were four cables, my friend. We are methodical, my men and I. To be absolutely sure there could be no slip, we strung four cables. Each one of them capable of detonating the explosive."

Mac struggled suddenly against his bonds. He saw that Cole and Smitty were doing the same, with sweat standing out on their foreheads. Mac saw The Avenger keep looking among the men as if for a certain face he hadn't yet seen.

"Four cables," repeated Addington. "Each led halfway across the river, to a sealed case in which is a contact clock. At 3:45 exactly, the clock hand makes an electrical contact—and that is that. It is now," he said, looking at his watch, "3:41."

"O.K.," said one of the others. "We know now that everything is all right. Let's knock 'em off."

Addington shook his head. "This Avenger is tricky. We'll wait till the actual explosion, to be sure everything is all right. When that comes—and it will shake this building clear across the river mouth—we'll let them have it. None of them must live, of course."

Benson spoke, voice unholy in its calm.

"The cable extends on from your clock device to this building?"

"Of course," said Addington. "The power comes from here."

"Then you could stop the explosion by throwing a switch here?"

"I could," said Addington, laughing.

"Then I would advise you to do so," said The Avenger.

151

For an instant there was such silence that you could hear the creak of Smitty's bonds as the giant threw all his vast strength against them.

"If you have investigated me at all," Benson went on, "you will know my methods. I avoid taking lives. I give the criminals I'm fighting a chance to save their own lives by surrendering. If they don't surrender, they destroy themselves."

The eerie silence continued while all stared at the icy-eyed man who seemed utterly helpless.

"I give you this same chance to surrender," Dick said. "If you don't, you similarly will destroy yourselves."

One of Addington's men said suddenly: "I don't like the way he says that. Gives me the creeps. Do you suppose—"

"Nonsense!" said Addington easily. "What could this beaten fool possibly do to us now?"

"You have a little more than a minute left," said The Avenger. "I urge you—throw that switch. Cut off the power from the explosive."

"You bluff magnificently," said Addington, bowing in mockery.

"Once more—throw that switch!"

Once more, Addington laughed. And then another member of his small army came in from the stair door, bolting it tightly after him.

This man was monstrously fat; he must have weighed nearly three hundred pounds. His heavy jowls were blue-black, with a growth of beard that would require shaving two or three times daily. He had mean little black eyes that looked at everything as if wondering how much profit could be squeezed out of that.

Smitty and Nellie exclaimed aloud as they stared at him. For they felt that now there was no doubt. They had seen the remains of this man after he had fallen forty-four stories onto concrete sidewalk.

Yet, here he stood!

"Got 'em all, huh?" the fat man said.

"All, Teebo," said Addington. He stood with his watch in his hand now. "And in twenty seconds—"

"Hey!" said another man suddenly. "The guy with the pale eyes! His voice! I remember where I heard that before. He was the guy in the mausoleum at Grayson Cemetery that said something about the mark of Cain being on Teebo's forehead—"

"Shut up!" snarled Addington with appalling ferocity that seemed without reason. "Five seconds—"

That five seconds seemed ten years long. And then it came. The explosion.

Shake the building? It did more than that. It seemed to pick it up and rock it as if lifted by a giant's hand. Mac groaned at the thought of its power at the source, if they could feel it thus at such a distance.

A sort of concerted sigh went up from all the big underground room. Addington put the watch away.

"All right," he said, a new tone in his voice. "It's finished. We've done it. Kill The Avenger and his friends—"

"Wait a minute!"

That was the fat man, Teebo. And his voice had a snap in it that startled Addington. The dark leader turned and found himself looking at the muzzle of Teebo's gun.

"What's the matter with you, man?" Addington blustered. "Why are you—" His voice died. The rest of the gang looked in bewilderment at the two of them.

"I'd like to know more about this mark of Cain supposed to be on my forehead." Teebo's voice was almost silky in its smoothness but sounded as sinister as a snake's hiss.

"Why, there's nothing to that," said Addington. "Mark of Cain! I don't know what—"

"Cain," said the fat man, "killed his brother. And I have a brother. Or had one."

"Perhaps Addington would like me to explain," Benson said. Behind him, his deft hands were working at his bonds. "Your brother headed the gang of picture thieves. You are in this gang. You brothers were the link between gangs, though your brother apparently didn't know that. He started to sell me 'The Dock,' and Addington killed him at the Pink Room of the Coyle Hotel."

A strangled sound came from the fat man's throat. His finger whitened on the trigger till Addington screamed: "Wait! Let me—"

"You said he wasn't dead," droned Teebo. "I kept asking you and you kept telling me. You said it was another guy went out that window, and that my brother was safe and hiding out."

"This man's lying," said Addington, with sweat pouring down his cheeks.

"He shot your brother with a silenced gun," said Benson inexorably. "The Pink Room orchestra was playing, and he must have made the report coincide with a drumbeat. Later, he was afraid the woman he was with either heard the silenced slap of the gun in spite of the drums or felt it strapped under his evening clothes; so he killed her, too."

"He's lying," panted Addington. "Look, now, Teebo, you aren't going to lose your head when we've just pulled off the biggest job in— Get him, somebody!"

The shot sounded as loud as another marine explosion, in the basement room. Addington stood for a moment with a hole in his head, and then sagged. Half a dozen guns leveled at the fat man—

A wild yell came from a man near the tunnel door.

"Hey, ain't this basement below the river level? There's water comin' in here! And it's comin' fast!"

The lights went out.

The place turned into an inferno as water shorted the circuit somewhere and plunged the room into blackness. The men had no thought of killing anyone, now, and no triumph at what they'd achieved. They were solely concerned with their lives.

The tunnel door had burst open. And down its slant from the waterline dock where the sub rested, water was pouring at a terriffic rate.

Smitty broke the last of the rope binding him. "Nellie!" he yelled, splashing through water toward her.

Mac and Cole felt a needle-sharp point go between their wrists and then their ankles, then felt their bonds slash free. The Avenger was loose, too, and was using Mike, the throwing knife, on the tough cord.

"Follow me," he said into Mac's ear. "Repeat to the others."

"Follow," was the word from each to the next, lips to ear.

Benson went to the stair door through which Teebo had come. It was high time; one of the terrified, almost witless gang yelled, "The door upstairs—"

The Avenger's fingers were as incredibly strong as little steel vises. He bent the bolt. No one would ever slide that back! He got away, others trailing him hand to wrist, just before the first of the maddened gang got there —and screamed in panic as he found the way barred.

Dick led them to a far corner. They stood in water up to their waists.

"Look," said Nellie, with practically no quaver in her voice, "if we have to drown so as to drown these rats, too, why—that's all right. But isn't there some way—"

"We won't drown," came Dick's calm voice in the dark. "The water will go little higher than this. Only the bottom third of the basement is below the river level."

"Not that it matters much," said Mac gloomily. "They did it. The *Carolina* and all those men—"

"Are perfectly safe," said The Avenger quietly. "I said I had rendered three detonating cables useless. That was true. But I found all four. The fourth I trailed back with me, along with the drum of explosive to which it led, to the submarine. When I rode the sub back, the drum rode, too, with wire paying out behind. I dropped the drum just before the sub berthed. The explosion you heard was not under the *Carolina;* it was that drum practically under the Gas Products' wharf, taking off the whole rear of the building and cracking the water-retaining basement wall."

There was so much to be said that none of his aides could say anything.

The Avenger went on, in an almost conversational tone: "The explosion will draw the river police here in a drove. They will take care of these maniac killers. It was not they who won, after all."

More than the harbor police came. They plugged the river end of the building, all right. But battering down the stair door came a dozen men from the F.B.I., trapping the gang in deadly pincers.

"So the lad was telling the truth," a Federal man said to Benson when the gang was rounded up.

"Lad?" asked Dick.

"A boy came staggering into the office a few minutes ago, with a lump on his head as big as a hen's egg. Said he had been knocked unconscious on his way and had just come to. He said to come here at once with a lot of men."

Smitty and Nellie looked at each other with shining eyes.

"There's a boy," said Nellie softly, "who is going to get anything he asks for."

But they felt silly, at that, about the Teebo affair.

"Are we dumb," said Nellie. "All we could see was what we thought we saw. Brothers! There are a lot of little differences between the fat man who fell from the Pink Room window and the fat man in that gang they're leading off to jail. The first one was a little younger, not quite so fat and had more hair. I don't see how you could have made such a mistkae, Smitty," she finished illogically.

"Me make it!" gasped the giant. "How about you? You were as dopey as I was about it."

They were still quarreling when they got to the amphibian for the trip back to New York and the Bleek Street headquarters. Then Smitty thought of a way to spike it.

"I'm in a hurry to get back," he said smugly. "We have such a charming guest—Jessica Marsden. She'll know a nice guy when she sees one. She'll willingly dance with me at the Pink Room."

"No one willingly dances with an elephant," snapped Nellie. "But you'll never have a chance to find out. If anyone is forced to suffer on a dance floor with you, it will be me—"

Her voice trailed away as she glanced at The Avenger. The rest were looking at him, too.

He was at the controls of the amphibian, pale eyes gazing straight ahead. He obviously hadn't even heard the banter and obviously was not sharing their jubilation at a big job well done.

A strange, restless mystery, this Richard Benson. All that was in his mind, now, was more of the same kind of dangerous work. More and more. Moving against crooks wherever they showed their heads, a machine of cold vengeance as if one man could whip the entire underworld.

Well, maybe one man couldn't. But he could fight till

the underworld finally caught up to him with knife or bullet. And before that day came, they'd know it would have been easier to fight an army than the one man, the pale-eyed, calm-faced, steel-muscled Avenger.